D0025364

THE CUTTLEFISH

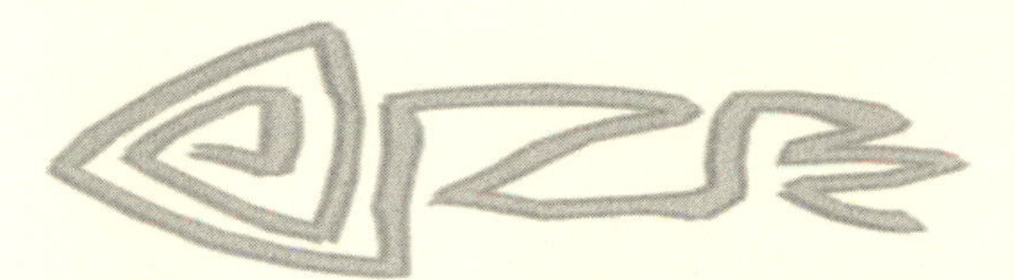

Also by Maryline Desbiolles

Une femme de rien

roman, 1987

Les Bateaux-feux

récits, 1988

Les Chambres

nouvelles, 1992

Quelques écarts

poèms, 1996

Les Tentations du paysage

poèms, 1997

Anchise

roman, 1999

(*Prix Femina,* 1999)

THE

Cuttlefish

A Novel

MARYLINE DESBIOLLES

Translated by Mara Bertelsen

HERODIAS *New York London*

Published by HERODIAS, INC., 346 First Avenue, New York, NY 10009
HERODIAS, LTD., 24 Lacy Road, London, SW15 1NL

www.herodias.com

Cet ouvrage publié dans le cadre du programme d'aide à la publication bénéficie du soutien du Ministère des Affaires Etrangères et du Service Culturel de l'Ambassade de France représenté aux Etats-Unis.

This work, published as part of the program of aid for publication, received support from the French Ministry of Foreign Affairs and the Cultural Service of the French Embassy in the United States.

Manufactured in the United States of America

Design by Charles B. Hames
Art by Ken Hiratsuka

LIBRARY OF CONGRESS CATALOGING-IN-PUBLICATION DATA

Desbiolles, Maryline, 1959–
[Seiche. English]
The Cuttlefish / Maryline Desbiolles ; translated by Mara Bertelsen.
p. cm.
ISBN 1–928746–21–7
I. Bertelsen, Mara, 1972– II. Title.
PQ2664.E743 S4513 2001
843'.914—dc21
00–054195

BRITISH LIBRARY CATALOGUING IN PUBLICATION DATA

A catalogue record of this book is available from the British Library.

Published in French with the title *La Seiche*, Éditions du Seuil
ISBN 2–02–033163–2, 1998

ISBN 1–928746–21–7

1 3 5 7 9 8 6 4 2

First edition 2001

THE CUTTLEFISH

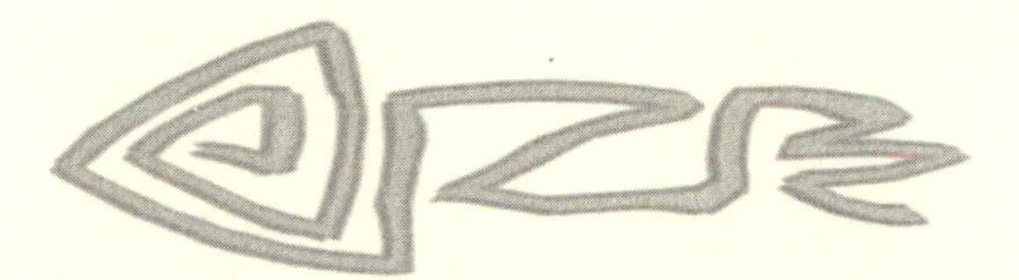

1.

Clean the cuttlefish taking care not to tear their bodies

THE recipe began with a mistake. I had taken care to copy it down exactly as it was dictated to me by the woman who reminded me of Cinderella's Godmother in the Walt Disney film, but the good fairy was convinced she had cooked stuffed cuttlefish. In fact, it was calamari, which I have often heard referred to as squid, but also inkfish, or even sea arrow, if you want to add a bit of local color. Was it not the way of this animal with its various names and fluctuating morphology to steep us in confusion right from the start? We have eaten calamari for cuttlefish, which are also called sepiola when they are small, or even Scipios, as I saw it written on the menu of a posh restaurant where someone was trying to be clever. There is a fine line between calamari and cuttlefish, but I don't have the slightest idea where the difference lies. I affirmed the initial error. My dish would also be called stuffed cuttlefish, even though I had bought calamari from the fishmonger who assured me, as he had only calamari to offer, that cuttlefish were much too iodic. Since it was unavailable, I naturally assumed that cuttlefish had some extraordinary qualities, especially since I liked its name and was already familiar with its famous, sparkling bone that, as a child, I had placed in a birdcage. I willingly resorted to the calamari, however, only too happy to discover the genus, an animal with a body like a pocket that is in fact called a mantle, a tentacled animal I had imagined preparing for tonight's guests. It was unthinkable to hold out for what I thought of as the exquisite cuttlefish, so impatient was I to get my project underway. I told myself that rarely were cuttlefish eaten (which is how we shall refer to the animal from now on), and I liked the idea that this comparative rarity would be, quite simply, stuffed with a filling that, to my mind, would be something benign and unpretentious. And so, I had the mollusks (as they are termed in the dictionary) tucked into a bright blue plastic bag with me on the bus headed homeward. I had hardly looked at them at the fishmonger's, barely cast them the casual glance of an expert who requires only a sweeping overview, had barely seen them, saving the pleasure of discovering them for our next and final tête-à-tête.

WHEN I unwrapped the paper that held them tightly together, the cuttlefish spread out a bit on the tiles of the worktable where I was about to prepare them. What struck me as they spread out was the fat-woman whiteness of their mottled skin. This certainly wasn't a blinding white. And besides, if it were the white of a fat woman, she would have been a sickly one. In any case, there was nothing left of the transparent, milky whiteness of the live cuttlefish I had seen a long time ago at the Monaco Aquarium. The truth be told, you could hardly tell it was alive, it was so hard to see. It took me a while to make it out behind the coral, where it hung motionless, pulsating. And pulsating it was, the tentacles and flaps and, above all, the cavity, which I perhaps incorrectly identified as its mouth. So, that big, rather disproportionate thing, swollen like a stomach, a little soft because of its flaccid contours, was actually its head. The cavity opened and closed so quickly you'd have thought the cuttlefish was suffocating. This frenzied state contradicted the graceful, languid mass of its body; it was too alive and yet not enough. I saw nothing beyond this cavity that neither sucked in nor spewed out, and for a while, I could imagine that it was incessantly, vainly, calling for help, without a hope of sound actually being emitted. Two women jostled me to get closer to the window, but they couldn't see the creature, perhaps more accessible to the rather low-angle view that my little girl size forced upon me. The ladies didn't waste time trying to find the cuttlefish. Countless delightfully shimmering fish were much more willing to show themselves here and there in the aquariums. The ladies said, "it must be ashamed," and moved on to the next aquarium laughing loudly. What they meant of course was that the cuttlefish must have been ashamed of itself, its ugliness, its shapelessness; but I understood that it was ashamed of us, or for those of us who wanted to look at it, or worse, those of us who looked at it when we never should have been able to see it. And even better, we never should have seen it, I understood, when I had my appendix out, which had caused among other things, the surgeon to burst triumphantly into my room after the operation declaring loudly that he had seen my ovaries, magnificent, in his opinion, and a beautiful shade of orange. I truly felt the shame I imagined the cuttlefish and I shared, shame that he could see my insides, show off with that, and most of all that he could see inside me the indubitable confirmation of my sex. Not only did I feel exposed, I felt confined, condemned to my future as a woman by the surgeon with the big gluttonous smile. I was twelve years old and already susceptible. It took me a long time to get used to that word *woman*, which included me since I, too, was equipped with all the ad hoc paraphernalia, including two magnificent orange ovaries. I knew very well that I was a girl and that I certainly would not turn into a man, but things were still fuzzy in my mind and I clung to this imprecision like animals cling to their shells, without which they would dry up in the sun. Mind you, I didn't have a strong tendency for lying, but if I had, it would have been more for the kind of invention that is a gratuitous lie, in short, a lie to make nice. Let's just say I didn't hate the truth. But it seems to me that we lose sight of it by exposing it so deliberately, that we lose the contours, even the flesh and its subtle variations, and are left with nothing but the blow that's been dealt us—a bit like seeing all black after you stare straight into the sun. I had the cuttlefish right in front of me, though, and much closer than the sun, drained of their ink, of the blackness and the whiteness that death had stiffened and distorted, drained of the weightlessness with which I had associated it. Maybe that's what growing up is: being able to eat what you were once ashamed to look at.

It's not surprising that a cuttlefish in trembling white will cloud itself in black when the time comes to protect itself. The fishmonger told me you could special order the fine ink that some people use to cook the mollusks. But for now, I want the cuttlefish in the fragility of its dubious whiteness and the subtlety of its white mantle, because when I think of something white, I don't think of milk, or snow, I think of those fragile, tiny, intangible white tufts that suddenly, with the help of a little wind, float miraculously around us and seem to announce springtime, cotton stars that descend to earth in broad daylight.

I HAVE all the time I need. I set aside the entire afternoon. At four o'clock exactly, as soon as the shop opened, I was at the fishmonger's. I returned home right away, my cuttlefish in its blue plastic bag. All the errands are done. There will be a stir-fry of artichokes à la Provençale, my stuffed cuttlefish served with spaghetti, then the cheese, and then just strawberries in season for dessert. Actually, I have no interest whatsoever in making dessert. What decides these things? You don't like the mountains, I prefer the sea; we both hate the harpsichord, you like to play ball; I'm no good at desserts, I don't have a sweet tooth. Is it intrinsic to our nature, as they say? Or is it our actions, like variations in the terrain, that make us branch off here, or turn there, and choose a certain path? Lord, where would we be without our tastes, what would distinguish us from one another? And do they really belong to us as much as we'd like to think? One day I was playing with my sister on the front steps. We lived just on the outskirts of town. Around us there were gardens, some left fallow, but still gardens rather than fields. I believe it was morning. Along came a salesman. He was at the foot of the steps, he said hello to my sister and me in a pleasant tone of voice, the tone of voice salesmen use. We were polite little girls, used to dealing with others. And suddenly, instead of saying hello to the stranger in turn, as I had been taught to do and as I had always done, I got my sister to turn her back on him and we ran away as fast as we could. I wasn't afraid, I was fleeing more to bewilder my sister, to take her by surprise, like when you make a face, I was fleeing more to play the shy, unsociable child that I was not, the little country bumpkin scared of her own shadow, perhaps like something I had read in a book. Needless to say, I must have enjoyed that sensation of fleeing, the freedom you get when you vanish from sight, so much so it seems that ever since that day, I like to slip away from others. It's a secret desire because I don't take the liberty of slipping away for good, but prefer to turn my back and choose to be alone. Maybe it isn't my nature though, but a habit I acquired the day I played that joke on my sister. We are so similar and call each other so often it's as though we know nothing about each another. Each one of us planted firmly on our own shore, and yet we call each other as though we were calling ourselves. But, habit or no habit, I am the one who invited people over tonight, as I often do, staking out a real plan of attack each time so the meal runs smoothly and the dishes appear like magic without my getting reddened cheeks or the haggard look of someone trying to prevail in hazardous culinary alchemy. Each time I prepare something I have never made before. I make it a point of honor of sorts and the uncertainty of producing something good sets the mood for my expectations for the evening. It may be a way of heightening the tension. I don't let my guests know that what they are eating is a first and that I'm slightly worried that the dish might not have turned out, might even be inedible, for I'm often inclined to take risks. I don't want them to see how hard I've tried, or that I am a bit nervous about the results of my effort, much less that I expect something from the evening. So, if, despite everything, a bit of my anxiety becomes palpable, I can always blame it on the qualms caused by my balancing act known as cooking. It's a cheap kind of lie to better hide the real reason. All I do is host dinner guests, which is a common practice, and there is no reason to make a big to-do of it, unless you want to run the risk of being taken for the hysterical type, or something along those lines, and I'm not too keen on that.

SOLDIERS undoubtedly understand the tactic of revealing one line of defense in order to divert attention from the real one. Of course, the trap, the decoy defense, must seem as real as the real thing. In that way it might protect something forever, something secondary, mind you, but something nevertheless. One needs something to sacrifice in order for others to believe in the sacrifice. Even when we lay down our cards, we're still in the game, and there's still strategy involved. I put on my big sky blue apron and meticulously wash the cuttlefish under the faucet. I amuse myself by filling their mantles with water, mantles that are now nothing but sacs, oblong and stiff, that I must be careful not to puncture. Once, it would have been out of the question to stuff the delicate and elusive body of a cuttlefish, but an edible sac of flesh lends itself magnificently to the task. I am cleaning and transforming that hidden mollusk from the Monaco Aquarium into garnishable seafood.

SOLDIERS undoubtedly understand the tactic of revealing one line of defense in order to divert attention from the real one. Of course, the trap, the decoy defense, must seem as real as the real thing. In that way it might protect something forever, something secondary, mind you, but something nevertheless. One needs something to sacrifice in order for others to believe in the sacrifice. Even when we lay down our cards, we're still in the game, and there's still strategy involved. I put on my big sky blue apron and meticulously wash the cuttlefish under the faucet. I amuse myself by filling their mantles with water, mantles that are now nothing but sacs, oblong and stiff, that I must be careful not to puncture. Once, it would have been out of the question to stuff the delicate and elusive body of a cuttlefish, but an edible sac of flesh lends itself magnificently to the task. I am cleaning and transforming that hidden mollusk from the Monaco Aquarium into garnishable seafood.

2.

Reserve the heads and tentacles

TRUE, the tentacles are still there clinging to the sac, the tentacles that adorn the head, which hardly looks any different, tentacle itself, a little bloated, two almond-shaped blots for dead eyes, like two tiny reservoirs as black as the blackest night, or rather, a night that has been snuffed out. The whole thing hangs at the opening of the sac like idle rope. That's where the mauve mottling of the cuttlefish's body is concentrated, as though all the bad wine we imagine within had collected there before it died. Does the cuttlefish actually contain bad wine, a kind of poison instead of blood, to scare us when it's alive or at least to disgust us, the cuttlefish and its clique of octopi and jellyfish? It's not so much its shapelessness, but precisely the miserable tentacles we are preparing to reserve that make us single out the cuttlefish. Of course, we're afraid of those multiple arms that could coil themselves around our limbs and lure us into the depths. A slightly primitive painting of a cuttlefish comes to mind on the lower part of the wall of a sumptuous ocean-front villa not far from Monaco, in Beaulieu, where the incandescence of the seaside charms was strongest for me, with the luxurious mild coast kissed by rugged cliffs that jut into the sea. I would have liked someone to take me to Beaulieu on every one of God's Sundays, to that turn-of-the-century villa-cum-museum, an aspiring replica of a Greek villa on the water's edge. That's where I wanted to satisfy my desire to learn, good student that I was, as if that place would reveal Greek civilization to me, but it was mostly the cleverly powdered melancholy of the place that stuck in my heart, a melancholy I longed to compare to my own, for mine was unnamed, inexplicable, and unadorned. Perhaps I wanted to cull from that so-called Greek villa the art of cosmetics without which you soon feel naked. I've forgotten almost everything about the slightly too delicate decoration of the villa, its murals that were a shade too pastel, its soft edges that acted as a poor defense against the rigorous salt of the sea air. I've forgotten almost everything except that little painting literally spurting up in my memory, depicting the curled tentacles of the cuttlefish wrapped around its wide-eyed head. There was no blackness to it, you could even say it was like the sun.

A LOT more goes on in cooking than in cosmetics. You are never as transformed as when you are cooking. Are we not, thanks to cooking, able to swallow what we were not even able to look at? All that dead flesh. Those cries, suffering buried in sauce. Sprinkled with fine and savory herbs. Garlicked. Strangled under the tongue to the point that even the words we use in cooking are contaminated by the transformations they denote. Words used in cooking do not mean what they say. *Reserve* obviously implies *cut*. I cut from the cuttlefish what is troubling and still moving, I sever its crowned head, I chop off its hair of dread and light like the hair in the painting on the patio of the Greek villa, I chop off its hair like the hair that hangs from a head lolling over the edge of the bed, swinging in light slumber after love, if you like. Seen from a distance, the hair of a woman in ecstasy, which, once you get closer, reveals its monstrous nature. Nothing smooth as you might expect, but a sickening tumescence, a rosary of suckers gripping the scalp. All those lumps, those blisters, in contrast with smooth, even skin. I have always been awed by (and have almost gagged on) the border between polished surfaces and those riddled with protrusions. Around the same time as my weekly, or at least very frequent, visits to the Greek villa, I sometimes had the same dream. I don't know if it recurred several nights in a row, or only from time to time, or two or twenty times. But it impregnated me to the extent that, from the age of ten, I remember as much (and maybe more) of this dream as of other events that took place when I was awake. In truth, it wasn't always exactly the same, the situations would differ considerably. But I remember it vividly as follows: I would dream of a woman, middle-aged, whose only distinguishing characteristic was her terribly ironic half-smile, so terrible that I'm sure it could still give me pause. This middle-aged woman with the unyielding smile was perched on top of a pyramidal throne. She gave me something inside a case: two spots, one a milky opal white, the other swollen, curdled and foul. I had to choose one of the two. My torment, which did not abate with each successive dream, was that I couldn't choose the right one, the white one, the one with no sharpness or edge to it (as though I was vaguely aware I would thus miss something), no more than I could choose the hideous one. I was drawn to the ugly blot, as unsightly as it was, and I fought to control my desire to choose it. I was gripped to the point of suffocation by a sense of regret for doing too well, and remorse for doing too poorly. And the terror, no doubt, of cutting myself in half.

It doesn't resist at all, it cuts very easily. I'm wielding a good knife, but a dull one would have done just as well. It is more difficult to cut meat even when it easily cooks right through, but it's the elasticity of the flesh of this mollusk, not its firmness, that I don't like. And then there's the worry that it might stubbornly become even more so. It's hard to imagine that it will end up tenderly giving way to our teeth. I am already promising to cook it a little longer than the recipe recommends. I can't help feeling edgy. A simple dinner and my hands are shaking. I hate myself for the excitement that crops up no matter what. Disproportionate, irrepressible, foreign to me, proliferating like a skin disease running amok. I hate myself for the fear my impatience causes me. Fear—more like vertigo. In certain moments of impatience, when I walk past an open window, I feel I could quite easily throw myself into the void in order to stop the throbbing at my temples and the tightening of my throat—a sort of overflow, strained at the elbows where it jams and is madly bent on bursting through—as if a water lily had grown inside and had spread like wildfire through my entire body. These images no doubt play upon those of my dream that night when big men appeared, headless (but without being frightening); they came up behind me, gently took me under the arms and with a light lifting movement, filled my entire body up to my neck, leaving only my head free, useless, dangling, and fragile like poppy petals in the wind. I also tell myself that this is the price I have to pay. Without this unsuitable, inappropriate impatience, without this extravagant, painful impatience that causes suffering, you wouldn't have its exact opposite, a kind of foolish devotion that makes the heart skip for no reason, absolutely no reason at all.

I THINK back to the villa in Beaulieu, to the cuttlefish joyfully ascending the patio wall, I think back to that villa steeped in kudos, built at the turn of the century on a prematurely old Riviera, on a Côte d'Azur that was already blighted, I always think back to that villa with the same effusion, as though for me, despite everything, the origins of the world were located there. Is it because of the sea so heavily laden with tales, the white stone tumbling into its waters; because a sort of innocence persists, put to a grueling test on every day God creates; because of the eternal light of the first day in spite of all that tries to obliterate it; because everything is always on the point of wilting and because everything still survives at the moment you least expect it; because this place is consumed by decay and yet compels our attention? Is that why I am so moved by this place, these beautiful places?

AND SO, the cuttlefish, burdened with stories, legends, and images, nevertheless keeps its diaphanous shapelessness as though it still hadn't chosen its genus, the waters still hadn't been parted from the waters, and nothing had transpired. The severed heads and tentacles make a nice little pile, pleasant to touch, pleasant to run fingers through. Of course, that's what cooking is too, making little piles and caressing them.

3.

Mince with 3 onions, 1 clove garlic, bacon, and parsley

NOTHING remains of the mollusk's indecision, or shall we say, the creature's imprecision, when it was still half hidden, half revealed in the miniature ocean of the Monaco Aquarium. Its so-called hair chopped off, its crown of night and light overthrown, heart wrenching like a toupee or a wig worn askew. Of course, that's what cooking is too, ridiculing what you fear. Death, first of all. Sometimes I think if you weren't cooking death, you'd have no sense of humor. We'll have to see. Perhaps there is less risk if we say that cooking is eating death. Consuming death, making it yours, masticating it slowly, savoring it, smacking your lips over it, eating death after you've severed its head, its skinned rabbit's head, bleeding slightly, the tongue wedged between teeth and two wide eyes, permanently bulging out of its head like the eyes of a madman. Eating death in the moment, whether it is mad or not, well browned on all sides until it is revived to a beautiful golden color, until it butters up a few onions and forgets itself in a touch of tomato. Is it because I still can't get this that I'm always a little generous with the condiments and use the widest variety of spices? Cook death, well spiced if you please, death that smells good and whets the appetite. As children we were fed poached brain, liver lightly seasoned in vinegar, tripe with tomatoes; we were fed death that was buried, death meticulously excavated and stripped of its delicacies. In our games, however, we ate for lunch only daisies, or sometimes chestnut leaves for fish, we ate in the sun, it didn't cook anything, it simply made our imaginary picnics possible and turned our handkerchiefs into white tablecloths gently spread out on the grass. We didn't have a sense of humor yet, only of happiness.

I'M having a bout of discouragement. The concoction of stuffed cuttlefish has only just begun and I feel like dropping everything and telephoning everyone to tell them not to come. There is still time, especially since nothing has been cooked, nothing has been permanently transformed, not even the cuttlefish, it's only been hacked at. So many meals have left me with the same taste in my mouth, first unacknowledged, then more and more pronounced, the same taste of incompleteness that has prevented me from sleeping even when my friends have stayed late. And perhaps especially when they've stayed late—the morning wasn't that far away—we had all tried in vain right up until the end, struggling in laughter and shared secrets, struggling, closer and closer together, struggling with the imaginary abyss that stubbornly sucked up our words and extracted all their juices. Our words fell back among us, desiccated and pale from never really having said what we wanted, as though they had slipped out of our mouths, invariably on a tangent, and dropped back among us, caught by the temptation that turned Lot's wife into a pillar of salt, our words freeze-dried forever, one might say, since we had no idea what water might reconstitute them. I had come to prefer social events, cocktail parties, art openings, at least I had no expectations. I get an incredible sense of lightness from not expecting anything. Anything that might happen gratuitously is a gift. I was happy about the tiniest complicity, evasive as it might be. I have come to prefer furtive discussions with strangers during trips; at a chance acquaintance's I would work myself up into feverish discussions with someone I would never see again. Back at the hotel, I would be a little ashamed of this debauchery of words, it seemed as though I had literally drenched my acquaintance with words, that I had flooded him. Recalling some of the things I said a bit too hastily, rather unnecessarily, I would feel a kind of retrospective panic. I felt I had started to resemble people whose gift of gab I found unbearable, and, I must admit, I felt I had lacked dignity, defiled myself. I had a choice between disappointment and disgust.

YOU mustn't rule out miracles. Once I was waiting for the bus in Rome. I had been waiting for a while when I turned my head and noticed a quite handsome middle-aged man staring at me. He was slightly off to one side, sitting on a low wall covered with ads. I was immediately struck by his distinctive appearance. The seemingly effortless way he was dressed, as if the pleasant combinations were mere coincidence, the way he carried himself, nonchalant but not slovenly, and above all, the way he appeared completely unselfconscious. So, even as he stared at me with an insistence that could just as easily have been crude, he seemed to be not somewhere else, but up above, although these words may not be appropriate since his manner was not at all superior, he was above as though he had lost his way and hadn't noticed. And I hardly dare say it, but I cannot stop this thought from creeping in, he was above us as though he were an angel, the issue of the sex of an angel was thus easily resolved, for there was no question about his virility, which was certainly distinguished and very accentuated. You have to believe that angels are the sex you want them to be. I caught his eye and he didn't hesitate a second and came toward me. He was shorter than I had thought, but lost none of his elegance once he was standing. Any crude or inappropriate thoughts completely dissipated as he virtually sidled up to me. He did not whisper, what need would he have had to whisper? The street was so noisy and those waiting for the bus along with me were not the least bit interested in us. I was nevertheless surprised when he addressed me as though he were picking up where small talk had left off. He said, "You are a real woman," a statement that did not fail to annoy me, the same way its multiple and often more underhanded variations do. It always reminded me of the surgeon and his orange ovaries. Not that I feel like a man, or even a man and a woman combined, but often times, most often perhaps, I don't see things according to my sex and I am, if not asexual, at least so elusive that no word could describe my state. But I had no time to give in to these thoughts, for suddenly the Italian added, "You are a real woman when, by some miracle, you meet a man." I did not burst into laughter at the thought that he took himself to be this providential man, I did not burst into laughter because I, too, had become an angel through the mysterious chemistry that makes you feel intelligent, beautiful, and victorious with certain people, and just miserable and colorless with others. I did not burst into laughter because I knew intimately what he meant, knowing how much only another person—an instant, a single instant, that is almost supernatural, I mean beyond the things we see as natural—could make what is referred to as femininity adjust itself perfectly to me, and make me a real woman, without shame, without embarrassment, without that gnawing feeling. We understood each other perfectly, the Italian and I, there was no need for any discussion, but we continued to talk about men and women until the bus came, which took a good ten minutes, and I too said things that were nice and stimulating, effortlessly finding the right words, since I was an angel and I was speaking to an angel, since we were talking simply so that the words would come, and flow like streams from our mouths.

At other, equally rare moments, the angel was a woman and her smile was free of all irony and her remarks were not double edged and perhaps her hair even undulated the way I like women's hair to undulate. I believed in these moments only as suspensions, for in no way do they endure or settle in, I believed only in these exceptional moments, but months, even years, could go by without my experiencing them again and foolishly, I couldn't resolve not to reach a precious agreement with my fellow humans, although we could hardly be distinguished from one another, laboring away as we do with our clumsy words, our heads in a bag. And basically, it really seems to me that angels could not appear, that words could not suddenly pierce through the fog if they weren't preceded by laborious effort, all those vague, annoying encounters, all the absurd display of intelligence, attention, love. It really seems that I could catch a fleeting glimpse of a painting of these repeated encounters, vain conversations, meetings, false starts, useless advances into which we nevertheless throw ourselves wholeheartedly, expectations and resentments, which, without our knowing, without our even suspecting such an occurrence, clear a channel for a few minutes' grace.

I MAKE a small bundle of the heads and the tentacles and place it on the cutting board. I mince it. I have a soft spot for the discrepancy I know by heart and that tonight's dinner will, yet again, illustrate: I am attached to a type of perfection that, without reason, I desire for something I don't believe in. Sometimes you find yourself building a castle just for shelter from a little wind.

Maryline Desbiolles THE CUTTLEFISH

I ARRANGE the ingredients with the pleasure of a child on the first day of school, taking her brand-new supplies out of her pencil case. The bacon (a little more than five ounces), the three onions (I hesitate between the yellow and the white, but not for long, for the white ones are fresher and shouldn't the white accompany my cuttlefish creation like the train of an imaginary dress?), garlic (I wrote down one clove, but I put in two, sometimes it pays to be generous in cooking, when it's not compulsive), parsley (sometimes I neglect to add it, sometimes I even forget. Aside from its color, and to be honest, that's already a lot, I have often thought that parsley doesn't have much of an effect on what I sprinkle it into, I have found its aroma a little weak compared to mint or divine coriander; but neither mint nor coriander can favorably replace it, they cannot replace it at all; parsley does not assert itself, it doesn't supersede, it doesn't even enhance, but it acts as a go-between, which, in cooking, is worth its weight in gold. Go-betweens build subtle bridges between ingredients that are not in the habit of meeting, in this case perhaps between the bacon, which we are more likely to view as hearty country food, and the iodic hair.)

WE rarely remember what we have eaten, though we may recall the pleasure we have gotten, or didn't, from the hosts, or even a snippet of conversation. But to taste cooking, and moreover, to actually do it, is a guaranteed way of putting memories in your mouth, mulling them over again, distilling what they are made of and not just having them rest on the tip of your tongue, but salivating them, putting them to the test of the tongue. Turned over and over in the juices of the mouth, the memories are there at the heart of the matter. The tongue of memory, the tongue that has become the center of the body, as it might in a drawing by a small child, the thin, pointy tongues of witches, the plump tongues of friendly fairy tale gnomes, the forked tongues that whet the appetite as much as frighten. I remember the gesture of a man who, as he nuzzled my hair, suddenly took it voraciously into his mouth. It was a gesture that was almost charming and yet a rare obscenity. It made my skin crawl with a combination of disgust and consent. He drowned himself in my hair as though it hung in long curls down to my hips, he lost himself in it as though it were at once a dark forest with radiant glades, he sank beneath it as though his greatest desire was to disappear forever. He was drowning himself. And so, I always imagine that women in love have hair that is long and wavy, especially in a dream, in a daydream where you become a lover held captive by her short hair, I always imagine that women in love have hair that is long and wavy, like the tumultuous water that can make you lose your footing at a moment's notice, as much for the woman who bears the river and lets herself be swept away by its irresistible current as for the man who is covered and uncovered to the point of vertigo by the imaginary hair. Only Pelléas saw the hair of Mélisande as boundless, filled with the song of the endless and deadly sea, whereas for Golaud, her hair was only beautiful.

HE drowned himself and he drank too. It was a drowning that profoundly quenched his thirst and spurred it on like never before.

I CUT the bacon, onions, garlic, and parsley into coarse pieces, then put it all together with the little pile of heads and tentacles; with my chopper I mince it as much as I can, as finely as possible. I could use the electric mincer, but I don't like the mush that comes out. Besides, I like the movement I impose on the chopper, a little awkwardly, for I use it this way only on rare occasions. My chopper, as vigorous as a sickle, joins in the fun; it is quite old, its little wooden handle is all worn, but its blade is flawless because I take care to have it sharpened regularly. Cinderella's Godmother, who wanted to get rid of it, gave it to me long before she had me taste her stuffed cuttlefish. She herself did not turn up her nose at mincing machines, food processors, or vegetable presses. And she always loved and admired cars, which had been a big event in her childhood. Her modern tastes ended there, however, for in everything else, her conservatism bordered on the reactionary. When I was a child and we were neighbors, I nevertheless saw her as the epitome of originality. She could have been my young grandmother, but she did things that other women her age did not normally do—not my real grandmother at any rate. She knew how to fish, recognized birds by their song, killed pigeons by holding their heads under their wings—suffocating them in their own heat—something which never ceased to horrify and amaze me. She was tiny and slim but didn't hesitate when it came to unloading construction materials her husband brought home in his big truck, and which they sold from the storage area under the house where swallows sometimes nested. She was very pretty and her little body was very well shaped. Everything about her seemed lively and firm, even her black, curly, or rather crimped hair—almost glistening, looking almost waxed—that she held back from the sides of her face with two invisible pins and some green scented cream. Most important, she cooked regional food; we were from elsewhere and my parents, who had just arrived recently, continued to eat as they had before. At her house, whatever was simmering filled the nose with rosemary and black olives, the sharpness of which was softened in the cooking process, at my neighbor's you ate raw vegetables swimming only in olive oil, which, exotic as it was, for me immediately became a must in all recipes. I fell in love with its marvelous color first of all, its sweet, strong smell, I even love it when it is rancid, a few splashes to flavor the evening's soup. I didn't ask my mother to change her cooking habits, but I never missed a chance to sit myself down at my neighbors' table, which I could just barely see over, greedily observing each one of their gestures, only rarely tasting one of their dishes, but latching onto all the words they used to name and describe them. But as soon as her gaze left her plate, or to be exact, the perimeter of her garden and the garden that was for her much bigger than the surrounding countryside, the neighbor became dishearteningly conventional. You could say that her views became narrower as her field of vision grew larger. As I grew up and began to take a look at the world outside the garden walls, I learned how much her conversation revolved around the commonplace, conversation that, until then, I had always found invigorating because I was captivated not only by her rich vocabulary (she took pains to speak excellent French) but also by the images and certain colorful pronunciation she used that were strange to me. I was delighted when she said *dace* for *days,* or the opposite, *zlip* for *slip.* She was a little precious when she said these words, sure that her pronunciation was right while everyone else's was wrong. And that's when something almost imperceptible took shape, and it took me my whole childhood to realize that she was a bit narrow-minded. I need to mince, mince as much as I can everything that ends up separating us, to find the little juice that spurts out, the juice that bathes unborn words, pre-word juice, juice we spit into the wind, as insolent as the first day we were confined, my neighbor and I, immured in our own wonders.

4.

Brown the mince in 2 tablespoons of olive oil; add uncooked rice (1 full cup), salt and pepper

LET'S move on to the serious stuff: the actual cooking, the surprise it always brings. I have often combined uncooked things, but what their mixture produces is never as surprising as cooking something you have seen raw. You would understand better if, for example, you made gooseberry jelly, if you gathered all those tiny red beads that seemed to contain nothing but a little refreshing tartness on very hot days, if you cooked them for a few minutes in boiling water, removed them from the water and wrapped the tenderized beads in a dishtowel that you then squeezed to extract the juice, if you mixed the red juice with sugar and put it back over the heat until it unfurled, filled out, and took shape, until several drops congealed on a plate to indicate that the jelly was ready, and all that was left to be done was to put it in jars, tender and tamed, sealing in the sweetness of those soft, tiny red beads.

TAKE the mince of garlic, onions, parsley, and angel hair. The hair of an angel, of a drunken woman, a fervent, blazing woman hysterically caterwauling insults from her front step, a martyred beast, a coy child who doesn't think you'll catch her if she hides under her unkempt mop, a demon, a rebel, a sleepy-head, a communicant under a white veil, a cuttlefish in an aquarium, partially revealed behind its forest backdrop. Or let us consider two tablespoons of olive oil (a little more, in fact, I let it overflow amply from the spoon, I feel the need to entangle the hair and its headdress of green), olive oil heated in a pan, not too hot, so the oil sizzles slightly. You toss the mince into the oil, turn it over and beat it with a wooden spoon, then lower the heat and let it simmer gently for a few minutes until it changes color on all sides. You can tell by the smell that everything has taken well, that everything has fully taken in the pan, while the slow aroma holds within its waft all sorts of familiar things, and some that are unfamiliar as well. Strangely, I think of lilacs, the scent of lilacs, almost the opposite of what is cooking, the opposite of the woven aromas that cooking concocts. The raw scent of the lilacs that lined the road leading to school, for they never smelled as good as they did early in the morning, thinly wrapped in the still sunlight like candies in transparent paper. Of course, by the time school was out we had forgotten them, our heads buzzing with stories to tell and those not to tell, stories we wouldn't even have known how to tell, of course the night was never long enough to wash out the large, outstretched bed sheet that suddenly snatched up all the words in the world, of course the night was never long enough to stop the scent of lilacs from surging within us once again in the morning, to stop us from becoming the water in a stream and its bed, from forgetting any resemblance to ourselves. The scent that made you forget everything is nevertheless the one I remember the most and when I smell it everything returns to its place, the house, the stairs that lead down to it, the little wooden gate that opens inward with a click the way the snapping of your thumb and index finger augur music, the road this scent embraces and cajoles with its wishes like fairies to a prince's cradle, and even the unknown, especially the unknown, that it opens and unfolds, so that for me, childhood becomes mingled with lilac season.

Maryline Desbiolles THE CUTTLEFISH

THE scent of the lilacs had no doubt faded in the afternoon and the teacher may have let us out unusually early, for it seems that I got home from school at an inappropriate time that day. It was very sunny; I left my book bag at home and ran to Cinderella's Godmother's house. The door was wide open, but the entrance was covered by a curtain of multicolored plastic ribbons that flapped gently in the breeze, brushing the ground with a soft little sound. I stuck my head in through the ribbons to see inside, but I had been blinded by the sun. I called out several times, to no avail. I hurried down the stairs to the storage area. I hoped to find my neighbor, but wouldn't have been upset if I hadn't because I was happy just to stroll around in the broad space that was packed with unusual objects, laid out in nooks and corners where you could make believe you were lost, like in a labyrinth (or the vague idea I had of one), according to the materials that were more or less sales worthy, with the less salable items built up into wonderful ramparts until the day a giant yard sale swept them away in one fell swoop. I stopped myself from calling out once again and stealthily crept forward like an Indian. Halfway into the storage area, my eyes accommodated to the shadows and I started to climb onto the platform when I noticed my neighbor behind the cement bags, desperately clinging to a man, she looked as though she was about to fall or that maybe she was trying to prevent him from falling. At any rate, they looked as though they were going about it in the wrong way and that both of them were going to fall. Their stance was so awkward I immediately felt like crying. But only for a moment because I quickly flattened myself against the wall, although I did have time to see the overcome face of my neighbor, whose hair, normally drawn back with four pins, was now disheveled strands of wavy hair sweeping across her fiery cheeks, loosened from the single pin that held them. If before she looked as though she were falling, she now seemed to be boiling over. I ran away as fast as I could, less carefully than when I came in, so I had time to hear my neighbor's worried voice asking, "Who's there?" but I was already out in the sun, which erased everything. I could have thought it was all a dream and I never said anything to anyone, but the sight of the disheveled hair was too vivid to stop bothering me, and from then on I paid even more attention to the coquettish care my neighbor took with her hair, which, because of a section of strands pushed to one side, because of the slack hold of the pins, had for some reason made her look like a madwoman.

I ALWAYS get a great deal of pleasure out of plunging my hands into rice and mixing it like gravel that also has the good grace of being good to eat. So much so that recipes with rice always make me smile inside. It wouldn't even surprise me if you pointed out that I wear a permanent smile at the mention of rice, no doubt because that little grain, even more than being destined to disappear into our mouths, served as the delicate pearly link between the Italian pronunciation of my mother's family name (my grandmother's risotto) and her birth in the Savoy to where her father and mother had emigrated in the twenties (the same grandmother's rice in a béchamel sauce). But it would have taken a mountain of rice to make the Savoy less foreign to me, to make it less foreign to the name of my mother, who made me love those rare excursions to Italy where we celebrated so much that I thought children never stopped dancing on tables there, to make it less foreign to the south where I was born and where I lived, where the countryside was certainly never as distinct as the green pastures surmounted by black firs, which were in turn crowned with white that I found simply heart-wrenching. To be honest, it was complicated, for the south was foreign to me, too. I never even managed to pick up the accent, only the taste, so close at heart to Italian. And especially the taste, I think, since I was not subjected to it, I think nothing could be worse than being subjected (and particularly to the infamous orange ovaries). Once the rice is tossed into the mince, it doesn't mix. The sizzling oil hardly has time to lap over it before the rice becomes like quartz and spurts out of the mince it will ultimately end up swathing. And so cooking teaches us how not to fear the foreign.

THERE will be couples here tonight. There will be the women of these couples, to whom I will force myself to talk in vain, as I will to their husbands who are also my friends. It turns out that these men I imagine to be so special have not married their counterparts. They have married women. I don't make anything of it because, I swear, I love the women, but they make me want to run away as soon as I sense they are convinced that they are any different from these men, men who sometimes live too large and whose wings they clip, these women who know, women who every day God creates, put their fingers on absolute reality, the naked truth, these women who are capable of keeping silent but also of thinking, or to finish off, of tossing out a word, one single, definitive, and biting word that leaves you speechless. Blue-bearded men are not the only ones who lock women in the cupboards of real women. Ever since the man who performed surgery on my appendix, I've met many surgeons who were women. I didn't sniff them out right away and at first I even gave them the full benefit of the doubt. A kind of mathematical illusion. If F. who is close to me chose that illusion as the closest one, then it would be closest to me too. But then they open the door to the room of the woman on whom they've operated and hurl some dreaded obscenity. Just like the woman of the couple to whom I had given, for the birth of their son, a book by a man who wrote enthusiastically about his own baby boy. Both parents sang the praises of the book, but she whispered an aside with a knowing look, "All the same, you can see that it was written by a man." Another time, a woman who, when her husband mentioned a project that seemed a little crazy but which you would say he'd put his whole heart into, rolled her eyes and sighed, as if to say, "You know how they are, you can't hold them back." I ask another if she would like a second child. I'm fond of her, of her good nature. Her back is three-quarters to me, she turns around and very gently says, "A woman never says no to that type of thing." That type of thing. Type. Thing. Close the door, gently if you please, so I can draw the sheet right up to my face and so I can swim, blissfully happy, between two waters, neither fish not flesh.

It took me a long time to accept the white of the eternal snow above the fir trees. Underneath the sheet, however, I made for myself milky waters, which contained a whole frightening and feverish world, so I could not ignore the fact that white, at least the white of the sheet, could be opulent. But I was even more convinced that white was not as dreary as I thought when I learned that my name, my father's name, came from the birch tree, whose silver-white bark makes it the most graceful of trees.

BUT careful now, it's a question of the mixture not taking, of the grains of rice not even browning but staying transparent, of it all maintaining an element of surprise when cooked as opposed to seeming vanquished. Another bout of discouragement. There is too much to do for so few shared words in the end. You simply have to complete what you start. That's without counting on the secret wish that everything be lost, that everything fail, be inedible, that everything look as though it came out of a witch's cauldron and you serve the stew sneering, the guests being unable to declare the good fairy good, which they would otherwise never miss the chance to do. The fairy is just a bit of a fairy just as the witch is just a bit of a witch. But what do you expect? This all-round rebellion is exhausting me. Meanwhile, this secret desire is drawing no more than the so-called exhaustion since the mince is turned a few more times with gusto and the grains of rice, more translucent than pearly at the moment, are dancing a jig at the bottom of the pan. And into the dance, let's give a few good turns of the pepper mill like the violent cook in *Alice in Wonderland,* sneezing the hell out of our countless inclinations to founder, to slide into the gloomy sea of muddled mince. Salt and pepper of course, so the salt is shaken without moderation, so our stuffing makes a mess out of diets, Lent, and other cold fish. So it is opulent, lavish, substantial, so that there is something imperceptibly excessive about it.

IT is because of this excess, so delicate (and the moment is even more so, delicate, for it is a matter of not slipping into excess that would mask everything and make you clench your teeth), that the mixture will not only succeed, but will even be remembered for a few hours after it's been eaten. You have to want to abandon everything so that, when you start over, everything begins to dance. It's a matter of seconds, for this little bit of turning and shaking could have just as easily left a burnt taste in your mouth.

5.

Stuff each cuttlefish ¾ full

I FOLLOW the recipe word for word and don't allow myself the slightest deviation. It's not like playing with fire. It's not about taking initiative, acting extravagantly or being imaginative. It's a way of brushing disaster with what's on hand, a way of taking the inside corner every day, of betting high with the low cards you've been dealt. What dress will I wear tonight? Here are the bodies of the cuttlefish, delicately sheathed in mauve, vaguely obscene, as they lie helplessly on the worktable. In the Monaco Aquarium, the cuttlefish was nothing more to me than a ghost, a cuttlefish soul over which a dubious white cloth must have been thrown, so that despite everything, there was still something to sink your teeth into, so that its name was not affixed to the label in vain. Who knows if I had thought that the bones given to birds were this soul hardened by death, in short, a stone soul of which the slow undulations I had glimpsed were nothing but a bit of dazzle, a rather crafty invention by the directors of the museum. But for now, the ghost must be stuffed.

THE stuffing is still steaming hot. I take a little in a soupspoon and stuff it into the cuttlefish, then I pack it with my fingers. Within seconds the tips of my fingers flush crimson and hurt, but I don't pay it any mind. I often burn myself when I cook, sometimes even to the point of getting blisters that I don't notice until the next day. One day when I was already a teenager, I was talking with my family about this lack of feeling and someone naively alluded to (naively, because they weren't trying to provide an explanation but just pointing out a coincidence) the terrible burn I inflicted on myself when, just barely walking, I fell into a basin of scalding hot water at the foot of my Italian grandmother's stove. It was a cast iron oil and wood stove (that my grandmother must have polished for I remember its shine) with a faucet on the left side for hot water. The water was running into the basin that she must have been filling, no doubt with the intention of giving my cousins and me a bath, when I fell

in headfirst. While my face, arms, mid section, and thighs were submerged in the basin, the boiling water continued to pour for a couple of seconds on top of my head before I was rescued, before my wool dress was torn from me, along with the skin of my chest. Only my ankles and feet were more or less unscathed, apart from a few splashes. It was thought, and not only by my grandmother who had me in her care and who, overcome with emotion and an overwhelming feeling of guilt, lost her ability to speak for many months, but also by the doctors at the hospital, that I would not survive or at best would be disfigured for life. I spent almost a year lying in a dark room under the almost constant watch of my mother, who stayed by me in a chair, where she even spent the night so as not to sleep too soundly. I couldn't open my eyes, which were nothing but living sores. And yet for as long as I can remember, I was a smooth little girl without a single scar. Family legend has it that one night my grandfather went to the mountains to find a woman who he had heard was a bit of a witch, and whom he convinced to follow him and succeeded in bringing all the way to my hospital bed. It was early in the morning and the woman asked that we be left alone so she could "call upon the fire." The secret gestures she carried out and the mysterious words she uttered provided an explanation for my miraculous revival a year later. The person who told the story was a distant relative who, along with the entire assembly of aunts, uncles, and cousins, thought I knew about the incident. But my memory of it was buried in darkness along with my wounds, and neither my parents nor my grandparents had ever been able to talk to me about it. Besides, I spent my youth too far from my relatives to ever hear about it, so I was completely unaware of my childhood accident. I was embarrassed and almost ashamed not to know anything about it, but I didn't let on and even pretended I was fully informed. I nevertheless asked questions, as shrewdly as possible, so no one would know how in the dark I was, and I swallowed the astonishment that scratched a bit where it was so tightly lodged at the back of my throat.

CURIOUSLY, I didn't hold anything against the people who hadn't told me. Whatever had happened, we were sharing this unspeakable moment that I relived in my own way by constantly burning myself, lightly of course, but so repeatedly that you could not shrug it off as simple clumsiness. After this revelation, I stopped burning myself for a while, but it came back without my even noticing. We didn't talk about my first baptism, which was known to have occurred, any more than we talked about the second, admittedly more brutal, painful, unexpected, which I had brought upon myself by running away from my grandmother as quickly as my first unsteady steps allowed, a baptism that I had administered to myself by way of a cast iron stove and a basin filled with boiling water, in which I could have literally left my skin, a baptism that came to closure not only with a miraculous recovery, but without leaving a trace, just as my grandmother recovered her voice without anything in her speech ever revealing she had once lost it.

ACTUALLY, I do have a mark from my violent baptism. It is minute and hidden under my hair. A hairdresser pointed it out to me many years later. It is a small, round, white spot on the back of my head where no hair grows, where no hair has grown since my childhood, a tiny, secret tonsure, a permanent clearing in my thick mass of hair that I immediately knew was the spot where the scalding water had continued to flow from the tap.

I LIKE the light sounds that are made when you stuff the mollusk, the smells that are given off, the strong scent of garlic, a little weaker than that of the onion, the moist scent of parsley and even the slightly stale but nevertheless operative scent of the rice cooked in oil, all mixed in with the iodic odor of the cuttlefish. I like to get my fingers full of it. It's a quiet moment when all you need to do is take care not to tear the flesh. You no longer ask whether or not this is all in vain, whether or not a healing word will be spoken, whether or not friendship between men and women is possible, whether or not certain women will continue to annoy as much, whether or not we might feel some resentment, whether or not it's possible for us to live with these searchlights that are flashed in our eyes and almost knock us senseless, so abruptly do they make us realize that one day we will no longer be stuffing the bodies of cuttlefish, world without end, and even longer.

THE first blinding searchlight I suffered was at catechism. I was seven, having attained what is known as the age of reason. This was when I learned about my wild fear of "world without end," the eternal black hole at the bottom of the earth, of nothingness forever. It was a reference to paradise during catechism that day that suddenly made me gnaw away at the certainty that dying was not an abstract notion that entailed disappearing into the air, in other words, going to heaven, but that it in fact meant no longer living. When the priest praised perfect order and the sovereign peace of paradise, I understood that the place where the dead go has nothing to do with the living world, that it is cut off from it, it is separate to such an extent that no separation I had endured so far could provide me with a clear idea. Paradise gave me the shivers. When I got home from catechism, I fell crying into my mother's arms and was quite incapable of explaining the reason for my unaccustomed outburst. From that day forward, I don't think I spent a night of my childhood without feeling the black hole inside me, its ineluctability and especially its timelessness (for which *world without end* ultimately offered only a superficial notion). This made me break out into terrible cold sweats and my heart beat violently to the point that I bit into the sheet to hold myself back, to stop myself from falling into the boundless, wide abyss.

THE little bellies are nice and tight, nice and pudgy, nice and bulging. The swollen cuttlefish are lined up on the worktable. Sometimes a bit of green juice drips from the openings. There is something comical about them and you cannot help but admit, something a little sad. Not that you get all emotional over the death of cuttlefish. In cooking, you never stop dealing with death, decked out in a way that it smells good and whets the appetite. It's their inertia that is distressing; it hovers behind the satisfaction of preparing a dish that is taking shape, for you cannot help but recall the graceful movements, the slow movements of a lover or a sleepwalker, the slow movements of a sleepyhead who has just barely left her nighttime slumber, her hair already tasting the light, her hair softly twining with the light and greedily tangling in it.

Maryline Desbiolles THE CUTTLEFISH

MUSIC? Certainly no music while cooking. Or only to prevent boredom when preparing the vegetables. And even then, that would be to deprive yourself of the knife's gentle whisper against the tender skin of the eggplant or the more rigid flesh of carrots, the light, but crisp sound of cleaning green beans, with delicate but brisk strokes on each side, and the obsessive repetition of these rustlings, murmurs, and tiny snips that help to soothe before the emotions of cooking and riskier transformations set in. For what a racket: sputtering, crackling, purring, whistling there is then, and oh, the beating heart. Music. At the time I left primary school, my favorite teacher was transferred to a distant town. The break-up was doubly hard. At the beginning of the summer holidays my teacher invited me and my family for dinner. The inappropriateness of singling out a student in such a way was no longer an issue. Not only was this the first time I shared a meal with him, but it was also the first time I had gone to his home to meet his wife and children. I was terribly excited. Waiting on the doorstep, for the teacher took a moment to open the door, we heard music coming full swing out of the windows, violent one moment and then soft the next, all at once harsh and feline, round and strident. Or rather, it was neither violent nor soft, neither sad nor happy: it was comprised of countless discordant movements all in the same breath, the breath of the composer, our breath, out of sync. Throughout the year, the teacher had made us listen to his records, which were certainly more accessible than this one, but I had not yet heard something that struck me as forcefully (no doubt the anxiety caused by the dinner invitation greatly enhanced this emotion). He sensed my agitation, and just before turning off the music and with the most pedagogical care, he told me in confidence, "It's Janáček." I realized much later that he had said Janáček, at the time I understood "Jan Assec" or something to that effect. The meal (prepared by the teacher himself, who was very mindful to spare his wife the task traditionally devolved to women) was so hurried that you could easily tell that he preferred music over cooking, or even that he had chosen music over the meal. It's true that the most astonishing precept our teacher had ever laid upon us, and that I had never managed to follow despite my eagerness to meet his expectations, was that one must always leave the table hungry. In the presence of this teacher with such high-minded ideas, I was ashamed to behave like a glutton behind his back as to be so unworthy of the interest he took in my scholarship. I had the horrible feeling that I was cheating him, since I couldn't admit that I always ate my fill. At least that night it was easy not to take seconds of the dishes he had prepared to music and I left the table and my teacher, since he moved several days later, hungry.

6.

Sew the opening shut with cooking thread

I HAVE never sewn while cooking and yet I discover some cooking thread in a drawer, no doubt purchased a long time ago for a dish I never ended up preparing. The notion of sewing is what amused me the most about the recipe Cinderella's Godmother gave me. Actual sewing annoys me though. Ever since I first encountered it in middle school, I found it highly unjust. Handiwork meant sewing classes for the girls, who worked like slaves, while the boys got to tinker with boards, glue, hammers, and nails. Sewing while cooking, with thick, almost string-like thread, seemed closer to the boys' puttering around that I had so envied. I found the task difficult, however, and even worse, the results uncertain. Sewing flesh together without any experience whatsoever seemed almost as improbable as sewing fog to the ground. I say this because during the week I dreamt I was trying to moor the fog. I don't know a lot about fog since it practically never settles here; and if I ever happened to come across some, real or in a dream, I felt its equivocal exotic charms. But the night we were on a road and had left the car, the fog was very thick. I say we, because I was with a man, but the fog prevented me from seeing him, even when we were standing side by side. Yet the way he thrashed around in the fog to find me, he must have been my lover. At times he managed to find me and I'd feel his hand on the back of my neck and right afterward he seemed so distant I could hear him calling me as though he were far atop of a mountain. But it wasn't irritating and even less frightening. I feel just as secure in fog as I do under an eiderdown, except that the fog doesn't weigh anything and it offers such freedom of movement that it leaves me completely giddy. The fog suited me to a tee. I made so much headway on that road, a road I couldn't see, I couldn't help but laugh. Just then the fog happened to break a little and I caught a glimpse of tree branch trembling like water and a flash of road that sparkled for a moment before the fog blanketed it once again. My lover galloped after me and gaily I urged him to catch me. The fog suddenly became speckled with sun and I felt the light would soon get the better of it. Then it began to lift slowly like a curtain, revealing the road and my lover's black shoes nimbly approaching me. I saw his shoes looming large and in great detail. I, too, would soon be revealed and I sank into despair. I started to pull on the fog with all my might, the way I would pull on a stage curtain, but there were only tatters left in my hand and the fog lifted unrelentingly to the sky while light swallowed it from above.

FROM the age of around seven or eight books taught me that true love should hurt, hurt tremendously; it didn't matter if a lover was ugly or rattled by tics, it didn't matter if a lover was disgraced—I had forgotten all that—the only thing that mattered was that he would sew across his chest, over his heart, a green ribbon belonging to the one he secretly, passionately adored. The stitching would become infected and, going over and over that scene from *Manon des Sources*, I imagined a hundred times, incredulous and fascinated, the strip of cloth and skin combined, swollen, bruised, and no doubt purulent. This is also what the pictures of Fabiola taught me, which I recall, I found about the same time in a forgotten box in my neighbor's storage area, and in which, for the love of God, one was voluptuously fried on a grill (the legend specified that the fat around the muscles sizzled), ripped to shreds in the arena by lions and bulls or thrown into the cloaca (a word I did not understand and constantly repeated) after having been riddled with arrows. Stéphane also taught me this. He never read a single book and he probably didn't even know how to read very well, so unwilling was he to learn. But he was in the same class as I was (a primary grade taught by a woman, it would be a while before I got to know the teacher who saw to the older children) and every day for months he discreetly showed me a dagger that looked enormous, and which he assured me he would use to kill me after class. I was so convinced of this that every day for months I conspired not to be stabbed to death. I asked my mother to pick me up or I had friends accompany me home under the most varied of pretexts, for I would never admit that Stéphane was terrorizing me, sure as I was that he would not hesitate to slit my throat in front of everybody; or else I made sure I was the first one out and ran full speed all the way down the road. I tried to convince myself that Stéphane, with his bounding gait, too preoccupied with his swagger, could not run as fast as I. To my great relief, Stéphane was often punished and had to stay after class. But then one day (I think it was after the Christmas holiday), our teacher announced that Stéphane's parents had to move away and that this was Stéphane's last day at school. I couldn't hear anything else, the blood was pounding at my temples. I pledged eternal gratefulness to I don't know who, since my prayers, no doubt offered up to all creation, were answered. I remained motionless and did not turn around like all of the other pupils to look at Stéphane, who was naturally sitting at the back of the class. When all the brouhaha caused by the news subsided, our lessons continued. Soon I heard a tiny whisper behind my back and my neighbor, as secretively as he could, slid me a piece of paper folded in four. He made a sign that it was for me. On it was written, *I luv u. Stéphane.* I turned without thinking to the back of the room and on the odd little face of Stéphane was the sweetest smile that had ever been given to me.

THE disgraced lover had *Manon des Sources* stitched literally through his skin. To the girl's ribbon, to her perfume, with that ineffable and precious something that it held of her, the disgraced lover had given his blood and humors. Sewing was no longer mending or patching up, but a painful and anxious form of alchemy that transformed two foreign parts, joining them with needle and thread into a third, a kind of heart in place of a heart, a visible heart that grows at the surface of the skin, beating no less than the other, palpitating with pus, an obscene heart, offered up even when the disgraced lover is dead, even when he hangs himself. So this heart, infected with suffering, catches in the throat of those who discover it.

SOMETIMES Stéphane's smile floats around me like the Cheshire cat's grin in *Alice in Wonderland*. But Stéphane's smile had none of the perversity of the cat's smile. It was a wonderful smile, the smile of the angel. It expected nothing in return. Despite our age and our failure to appreciate things of love between men and women, it was a smile of love. As though the mouth of the little tough guy, the budding bandit, had become unstitched. Mum's the word and mouth sewn up tight. The note Stéphane wrote to me had untied his mouth. Give me just one word and you will be cured. You could say that Stéphane discovered how to breathe and that made the unhoped-for smile bloom across his face. You might say he had never smiled before and that he was saving the blossoming for me, for a time when he would have told me everything, when his words of love would have been delivered, when I would know that his death threats were nothing but their silent opposite. You could say that he had never smiled before then. In our class photo, which I still have, he is standing several rows away from me, slightly blurred as though he couldn't stay still or was even trying to escape; his small eyes are malicious, his face a little long and his mouth strangely, almost violently, shut like a ruffian who is being questioned by the police and doesn't want to let the cat out of the bag no matter what.

ONE long needle with a large eye, thread like fine string. I imagine so clearly the impossibility of this working that I am already planning solutions for recovery. A split second of panic. It's ruined, absolutely nothing will work, the little sac has to be sewn tight or else it will be shapeless and disgusting. What have I gotten myself into? To my surprise, the needle slides as if through butter and by the third stitch I can already see that the edges of the orifice are joining together perfectly, that the thread is uniting them admirably, that everything is working out with disconcerting ease, as if the flesh of the cuttlefish had been created to be sewn. You experience a joy, oh yes, joy, since the orifice is now fastened shut (a bit of filling dripped out while you were sewing, but barely, and you'll do even better with the second little sac), since you hastily stopped stitching, gaily, for this type of sewing has none of the minute challenges of sewing cloth as an exercise to kill time; you experience the joy of soon aligning the little sacs with their bellies gently touching (you can feel the rice, still hard, through them), of course, in the back of your mind you think of the gaping wounds you might have sewn on the stumps of limbs, so roughly that you would have done so under exceptional circumstances, surely war, what will I wear tonight? No, not that dress, too fancy, it's a night with friends, I don't need to flaunt my tiresome willingness to seduce, what nonsense, but then again, why not?

7.

In a saucepan, sauté 2 chopped onions in 2 tablespoons of oil

Oh, I'm tired, so much uncalled-for excitement, I'd like everything to have been eaten, everything to be done and done well, so I can curl up in bed with a book. I know all too well that even if everything goes smoothly, it will not be as perfect as I would like it to be. It takes courage not to fear imperfection. Courage every day God creates not to fear that all our debauched gestures, all our comings and goings, all our words, our specifications, despite all our efforts, scarcely belong to us. Scarcely resemble us (for our mirror image is what is considered perfection). Not only would it take courage and more than courage not to fear it, but even more to rejoice in it. We always flutter like the nearest windward sail, continuously hesitating between dead calm and the gale force that would finally fill us for good. Yet we remain on the windward edge, in this state of agitation, this flapping of wings that drains us of our strength.

THE taut little bellies are waiting patiently on the worktable. They are ridiculous and heartwarming. The state into which I have put them forbids any shilly-shallying or any frame of mind that might botch their final transformation. I take out my reddish-orange cast iron saucepan, nicely oval-shaped, brand new, since I convinced myself that one could not pride oneself on cooking without a cast iron saucepan. It is an exact replica of the one my neighbor always had (except that hers was black) and in which simmered, among other goodies, lots of pigeons prepared with olives. Although this saucepan is new, my memory is seasoned with all of the aromas that wafted from my neighbor's, mixed with those that wafted from my mother's saucepans, forming an indecipherable bouquet. Ever since I have happily endeavored to remember each one of its petals, those aromas and the salivation they gave rise to, with the colors tossed together, the sound of what's caught in oil, what simmers or cooks slowly at cruising altitude, aromas, salivation, colors, sounds, whose remanence fully participates in these famous tricks of the trade. I chop two nice yellow onions on a wooden cutting board, crying profusely as I should.

I COULD imagine that, if truly unavoidable, she might have cried while peeling onions, but certainly never out of sadness or anger. In the class photo with Stéphane and his little hooligan face, Claire is smiling; it's a radiant smile, but she is not smiling at me or the photographer or anyone, she is smiling at the world. I don't think I talked to her much, I don't think I played with her often, but I loved her. And I felt I loved her from the joy her smile brought me, her smile that opened even further her open face, with its well-defined cheekbones, and her straight, very blond, almost white, hair where a barrette danced. Claire always had messy hair, which only added to her charm. She was certainly not very pretty, I believe her features were a little coarse, a little ill-defined, but all I had to do was say or hear her name, Claire, tied to the foreignness of her last name, Masterenko, Claire Masterenko, and I'd feel the light of snow, the light of a strong wind that reddens the cheeks, the light of the sky above, incredibly clear, all kinds of light from everywhere, a showering of light from the horizon as far as the eye could see, infinitely mutable. I was especially dazzled when she sang. Her voice was so in tune with her name that I was stunned each and every time. Claire's voice, which never cried, made others cry with joy. The clear spring she sang flowed from her mouth, from between her full lips, flowed up from under her teeth like so many pebbles polished by fast-moving waters, sprung from her secret throat. Claire's mouth was a clear spring. She was the only one I could hear as we laboriously tried to sing rounds, but the teacher would often ask her to sing solo just for fun. In the last row of the photo, not far from Stéphane, is Claire's brother, who was as slow as Stéphane was quick, as lumbering as Stéphane was unable to remain still. Claire's big brother was very slow, he was years older than his sister, but found himself in the same class without it bothering him in the least. Mentally retarded though he was, she held his hand as they walked home just as you do with your elders. I can still feel the shame I felt watching him laugh stupidly with his mouth open. I was frozen by his simpleton laugh, when the teacher asked him what those bumps were on his hands, when she cruelly insisted in front of all of us, the younger ones, who were looking at him, the simpleton, with his head always flopping to one side, clumsy in his big body, out of place in our younger class, when the teacher ended up answering for him that fleas were what caused those bumps on his hands and that he was dirty and that she would no longer accept him in her class if he continued to be covered in flea bites, as he returned to his seat, still laughing his mute laugh, the older brother of the luminous Claire Masterenko. Claire and her brother lived with their mother (a large, fat woman, as ugly as sin, just as ugly as the cook with the pepper mill in *Alice*) in misery and filth. I walked home with her once, we hadn't thought about going in and I didn't notice the place, so enthralled was I drinking in her bright smile. But faced with the humiliation the teacher inflicted on her brother, I realized that the place where the Masterenkos lived was just this one blind room that opened onto the street, a dark cellar where their strange blondness had managed to blossom. Claire's voice, the clear voice of Claire, seemed all the more precious to me when I learned that she came from that hole.

CLAIRE'S clothing and her heart-warming messy hair were often drenched in the slightly nauseating odor of the cooking her mother managed to do their cellar. Although her mother looked like a scullery maid, you could nevertheless see in the rosy, chubby cheeks of her children, in their same gobble-hungry lips, that she fed them as best she could. Judging by the odor her children gave off, the mother must have made a lot of fried foods, for in the morning you could smell on Claire what she had eaten the night before, which always seemed a little heavy and fatty, curiously mixed with the smell of the milk she drank, with her little girl smell, which sometimes still reminded you of the smell, so pregnant and sweet, of a baby, and with the delicate smell of sweat, since she often ran as fast as she could to get to school on time. She always seemed to awake at the last minute, her eyes all hazy, still focused on the warm night she had just left behind, the edge of her plump lips still wore the trace of the milk she'd downed in haste, and her hair poorly held back by a slightly gaping barrette did not hide the fact that she had just gotten out of bed. By her wrinkled clothes, you could even imagine that she had slept in them and that she arrived at school with the night on her shoulders in such a way that her smelly, wrinkled, worn clothing was laden with stories that bespoke nothing of ours, always fresh and impeccable. She had on us the superiority a woman of the night would have on innocent young things or a city traveler on country folk. But she was unaware of this superiority. And although I may have envied her old blouse, a hand-me-down or one her mother had bought in a second-hand shop—that was of such a worn blue it gaily passed through all the subtle nuances of the wrinkles it underlined—Claire envied no one anything for she sang like water from a spring.

Two tablespoons of olive oil (the recipe doesn't say what kind of oil but there is no thought in my mind of using any other kind) in the saucepan that is trembling ardently. The onions are tossed in and they're singing too, like a bunch of angry devils. Strange that out of these moments I recall only Stéphane and Claire, surely the poorest in the school, whose parents came to our village for a while to hide their misery and to try to regroup before leaving once again. And Claire, like Stéphane, soon moved on, leaving behind after her short stay the gift of her smile, an involuntary gift, like the unexpected smile from Stéphane the ruffian, Stéphane the rebel, the gift unhoped-for among them all. I wasn't really aware of their poverty, we weren't very rich ourselves, but I think I knew they were on the fringes, that they were hopping on one foot along a precarious edge that could give way underneath at any moment (one day they disappeared and I never heard from them again). I don't remember Stéphane's parents, if they even existed, but didn't Stéphane live like a young fox in a foxhole, abandoned by everyone, owing nothing more to his father than an enormous dagger and to his mother only a long-forgotten smile, with which he ended up, *in extremis,* rewarding me. Claire and her brother lived only with their mother, I had seen her, their sturdy mother with the jutting, gapped teeth of an ogress, a woman so big and bulky it was not completely impossible that she had bypassed men altogether to make her children, a kind of monstrous goddess, whose children had perhaps come out of her ear, blond and smiling. We were so close, Claire and I, we could touch each other often if only to catch roughly or push each other in line, and we hardly knew how to talk to each another, but then it wasn't necessary to tell what we knew about ourselves, we were still so happy to recognize that we were similar. Why dig deeper into what separated us by even one iota and which would grow beyond measure, much more than we would, to prevent our slapping each other on the back and larking around together? It pulls at my heartstrings to remember Claire Masterenko's bright voice, just as it pulls at my heartstrings to remember how Stéphane's smile had erased in a second all the terror he had caused me. This pair of little bumpkins performs a sprightly dance, forever irreplaceable and incomparable, out of reach, forever caught in the smallness of childhood, so that I have a hard time fitting Gulliver into Lilliput, my little pair of bumpkins, overtaken by a ghostly pale that already almost completely erases them, except sometimes, rarely, thanks to a mysterious opening, the breach that suddenly gives them back their color.

8.

Remove sautéed onions from saucepan; brown the stuffed cuttlefish with the remaining olive oil

THERE is no point in doing everything as though your life depended on it, I was judiciously advised one day. At the same time, I told myself, what is the point of doing anything if your life *doesn't* depend on it. Incurable. A whole life spent wrestling with niggling likes and dislikes so that they belong truly to no one but ourselves, so we can say we are who we are and no one else. "You like to wear this color with that color, how original!" "You don't like potatoes when everybody else likes them. A childhood trauma perhaps?" "Horror movies? That's interesting, you know, when it comes right down to it, I don't think I like movies." A whole life spent sweating blood and tears to differentiate ourselves, to try passionately to distinguish ourselves, to push our heads above water and wave our arms around until we get so exhausted by this strange and difficult move that we get cramps, we almost drown, we do drown. Fine. The little bellies, nice and bulging, nicely sewn up, are waiting on the worktable. The onions, nice and browned, almost translucent (as though they have become soft amber-colored glass), are waiting in the casserole. Everything is in order.

ONE night on a train, it was a thick, heavy night, sticky, it wasn't one of those nights when you feel etched, when unpronounceable words you have in your keeping begin to twinkle in the darkness, not one of those nights when it seems that things and you are well defined, when it seems as though everything is starting to break out into meaningfulness (like you would say a fire breaks out); and yet without your knowing which, not one of those nights when you think you can conquer mountains, it was a night that weighed on you with all the weight of night, it was a night that clung to the slightest movement, as you turned over and over in your berth, unable to sleep. In the compartment, a young mongoloid girl and her parents are sleeping or pretending to sleep, and above me, a beautiful brunette woman. It's a summer night, the train is an oven. The young mongoloid girl made sure that everything was hermetically sealed, the window, the curtain, the sliding door, the compartment was unbreathable. The apologetic looks the parents addressed to the brunette woman and me, as an appeal for their daughter, did not allow us the least remonstrance. The three of them thus plunged, the girl with great delight so it seemed, into the thick, horrible night-time soup. The brunette woman and I remained standing in the corridor as long as possible. The presence of this woman was comforting, but I nevertheless found it hard to keep up conversation. I was tired and didn't have a lot to say to her. The woman was no longer young, fairly tall, and almost stout. She was very beautiful with her steadfast blue eyes of a strange, ultramarine blue that was not at all transparent, with a chignon that she wore high on her head and that was so voluminous you could well imagine she had very long hair. I would have liked to have spent the night in the corridor with her, saying nothing or next to nothing, leaning against the window with her, watching the night pass by with slivers of lights here and there or the faint outline of the stations where we stopped. But the brunette could not bring herself to accept silence and the unsuccessful conversation exhausted us to the point that, despite everything, we ended up going back into the compartment to try to sleep. It was even worse than we could have imagined. The gluey night strapped us to our berths and we lay there floundering weakly as if we could fall asleep by struggling, but of course sleep never came. Far from gently rocking us, the monotonous song of the train seemed to drive the torpor right under our ribs. The night light must not have been working, and despite the efforts of the mongoloid girl's parents to block out everything, a bit of light filtered under the door so you could vaguely make out the sleeping shapes of our traveling companions. Their closeness, and the slight agitation this caused me, kept me even further from slumber. I resigned myself to the fact that I would slowly cook, wide awake, in that somber oven. But all of a sudden I was wrenched from my torpor. I didn't know right away if someone had touched me or if, among all the other sounds, a sudden noise had alarmed me. In vain, I open my eyes as wide as possible. At first I can't see anything but the night wildly dancing with the lurching train and then, this time without a doubt, I feel a hand trying to latch lovingly onto me; I see the brunette's long hair as she leans over me, her immeasurably long hair that she has let down for the night. I am very frightened, not only because of the hand awkwardly pulling me toward it, but also because of the hair, itself blacker than the night, black sun, sun of sorrow, contaminated water flowing toward me to coil around my forehead, my neck, my shoulders, my stomach, my knees, to whirl me into the depths. I am frightened and disgusted, as though my mother (the brunette is about her age), who has lost her mind and no longer recognizes me as her daughter, has mistaken me for another woman or more likely for another man and is trying to seduce me. I push away the hand more fiercely than necessary, but before it disappears, I once again see the hair moving languidly like a funeral veil with no other purpose but to fan me, I see gloomy algae gently swaying and I hear the rustle of the breeze in the tall trees like sweet, fresh music, a song you could whisper in my ear to put me to sleep, I hear the song of mermaids hoisting themselves up those silky ropes and instilling in me a tiny yet nevertheless persistent regret and sadness, as secret and relentless as the pulsing of the blood in my veins. And yet it is this sadness, this obstinate pulsating sadness that, strangely, ends up putting me to sleep.

LET'S put the cuttlefish bodies into the pan. There they are, nice and tight and sizzling in the olive oil that slicks over and browns them. A bit of hot oil spatters on my hand, but I hardly notice. Haven't we suffered through a thousand deaths before, finally facing the fact that these little hardships are what they are—mere trifles. My skin has kept no trace of the ferocious burns I don't remember, so that I really don't believe in them, there was probably some mistake, it was all an exaggeration. My skin swallowed up the pain and the pain disappeared into it as into a large bucket of milk, without so much as a bubble on the milk's surface. Sometimes I imagine that the pain had nonetheless hardened, a large egg floating inside my body, I imagine that it will eventually lodge somewhere, graft itself to a part of my body that it will inexorably rot, sometimes I imagine that it is in my throat and prevents my words from flowing freely, sometimes I imagine that its presence elsewhere is less noticeable, that it is maneuvering oh-so quietly, I don't know what it is invading, what its movements are destroying, I think it must have first wounded what is most tender, but the rest will not be worn out by the constant squeezing, flattening, shaking of the intruder, the big loathsome egg, the monstrous cyst that enshrouds the pain, that unknown pain, which was nevertheless my closest companion for months. Is it possible that it had disappeared as purely and simply as the scars on my skin? Sometimes I imagine sheer madness, that I forget my burns like I forget my birth, a point in time, that's all.

SOMETIMES I imagine that the brunette on the train could have driven out the egg of pain, I imagine that she could have sensed its hardness, the imperceptible protrusion that she would nonetheless have discovered with her fingertips. Sometimes I imagine that once marked out in such a way, it could have been coaxed, that egg of pain, made to stay still, stopped from wandering around the body it was gently ravaging and, by coaxing it, confined it to the spot where it would have been discovered by the brunette, so that it would have spoiled just one spot, and, encrusted there, would stop its ransacking; at least then I would have known what I was up against. I don't know why I have invested the brunette with such power. No doubt because of the comfort her presence brought me in the corridor and, even more, perhaps because of the secret distress her incessant and almost desperate babbling revealed. I believe her empathy would have led her hand to the pain. And so, with her hair undone, with her magnificent hair spread out, she would have tenderly hidden from the world, she would have hidden from the night what she had found. Of course, it is the memory of the brunette that brings on such dreams, but also the memory of the stifling night in the compartment, that night in the incubator when anything could have happened, the most unimaginable thoughts and movements, that night in the incubator that could have quickly fomented what until then had been kept at bay. The memory of the brunette, but also the memory of that suffocating night and the person who had wanted it, the young mongoloid girl, more than a deformed image of myself, for I had the feeling I also carried her inside me, the retarded child, from that night before night, that boiling night before the dawn of the world.

THE surgeon who took out my appendix when I was still young demonstrated an exquisite sense of discretion by not mentioning he had seen the large egg he hadn't been able to grasp, tangled as it was in my delicate organs. Truth be told, the surgeon who had seemed worse than an ogre when he discussed my ovaries had done so deliberately, to talk about something else, to turn the conversation, as they say, away from the crucial point to avoid shedding light on something much more secret than my orange ovaries. In my digressions I almost feel a fondness for the man who chose to pass himself off as a dimwitted brute rather than reveal what was hatching inside me, yes, there is almost a fondness and gratitude for the man who restricted himself to the garish color of that which established my femininity rather than divulge the enormity of what had developed inside me, the monstrousness of the intruder that for him was the basis of my strangeness and no doubt my madness. The foul egg was what was obscene, not the orange of my ovaries. I was the one who was indecent, carrying around such an aberration, not the surgeon who had chosen to emphasize my glaring normality, to announce what linked me unquestionably with life, even what certified that I would be able to give life, and who had kept silent about the egg of death that had hatched when I was at death's door, a hair's breadth away from the realm of the shades, which is indeed far removed from color and even further removed from the color orange; besides, the egg must have been dirty white, dishwater gray, a color that was not a color, as though it were embalmed, stricken. The smile I had found carnivorous and boorishly triumphant was in fact a rallying cry to the world of the living, a sign to encourage me not to let what plagued me get the better of me. I hadn't understood a thing, but I had unwittingly swallowed the smile that for a while had held the egg in check, unbeknownst to me. I remember waking up after the operation, a painful memory, I had a hard time pulling out of that terrible sleep, sleep they had injected into my vein and which I had resisted tooth and nail. When I awoke, my fear and useless resistance had awakened intact. According to my mother, the entire night after the operation I jumped around in my bed, I kicked, I rebelled against that inflicted sleep; but wasn't that sleep how I had rejoined the encysted pain, wasn't that artificial sleep what opened the night I carried inside me, wasn't I rebelling against the awakening that would plunge me back into ignorance, into the night of my night. I believed in it for a while, for a while I believed in the egg of death.

Maryline Desbiolles THE CUTTLEFISH

LET'S get back to our cuttlefish. Though that's just a manner of speaking, for I had never let the cuttlefish out of my sight, they would have burned, nothing would have worked, nothing would have turned out if I had thought of something other than the cuttlefish, other than the dish I'm preparing. I am fully engrossed in my cooking, for cooking is what puts words to my memory, my dreams, it's through cooking that I remember and let my mind wander. Another dish would have brought back other words. Another dish would have made me anew with other stories. Another dish would have given me another life. It's as though at the moment the cuttlefish are enveloped, delicately protected from the world where they once undulated. They have nothing to do with that world anymore, nothing to do with their sisters with the long, disquieting hair. Now they belong to us. In no time they have taken on that golden-brown color that cuts them off from the dead. They are no longer dead, they make us hungry. We have taken possession of death. We have gilded it. There is nothing left to do but place the stuffed cuttlefish in the casserole where the onions are murmuring. They, too, have forgotten where they came from. They no longer belong to this earth, they have taken on the transparency of clouds drawn through sky. So much so that their gold mixes with the clouds for a moment.

9.

Flambé with cognac

A FEW days after I was told about my accident—when I could barely stand on my own two feet and that had caused me to burn and peel like a chestnut—I went to pick up my silk dress from a dressmaker who had recently set up shop in the old part of town.

When I brought in the dress for a few alterations, one of my cousins had come along, a very pretty girl who could not have been much older than four. The dressmaker had just fixed up what for a long time had been a grocery store. Fix up is a bit strong, perhaps, since what served as her workshop seemed more like a construction site or a makeshift shelter. The place would have appeared ransacked and in frightening disorder if it hadn't been for the formidable presence of the dressmaker who had what it took to shoulder all that neglect and turn it into something sequined, ethereal, so that it actually made us smile. The heavy iron blinds were drawn, only the small door through which we entered was ajar and what was once a shop now resembled a she-wolf den. Mountains of clothing were its only decoration, and the furnishings of the vast room consisted of the chair she was sitting on and the table where she worked, where the sewing machine shone brightly under the lamplight. The she-wolf was very fat, her mouth very red, and her bosom most opulent. She hungrily watched us approach, especially as my little cousin approached, as though she promised to be a delicious feast. But the little girl wasn't afraid of the twinkling eyes of the fat woman, she even began to laugh. The dressmaker made us feel happy that we were appetizing. I was alone when I returned for my silk dress and didn't realize right away that the workshop, once simply in a state of neglect, was now completely devastated and gave off a strong smell, an odor with which I was certainly already familiar but didn't recognize at first. The room that I had seen as a dark wolf's den when I had come with my cousin was now horribly black. Everything had burned. The acrid smell of a fire that had been drowned under streams of water still caught at the throat. The fat woman appeared, magnificently pale in the midst of the disaster, even her lips were white. I had never seen her standing before, she stood a head taller than I, her hair pulled back, she was magnificent and soft like a hill in the middle of the prairie. She told me soberly, "there is no more silk dress."

SOMETIMES we are so blind and deaf. I made no connection at all between what I had been told and my dress disappearing in the flames. So I couldn't comprehend the exaggerated pain I felt, I, who was generally much more flippant and forgetful. True, it was a present from my mother, true, it was an expensive dress, true, it was one of my favorite dresses, true, it was unpleasant for me to imagine it carried away in a flash by tangled strands of fire, and yet none of that could explain my being so upset. But I saw nothing, blind and deaf, my head in a bag. It's true I could not bring myself to believe the story of my accident I had been told in passing, I could not bring myself to believe that it had really happened to me. And even today I make no connection at all between what I was told and my dress disappearing in flames. In fact I am right. In fact there *was* no connection between my silk dress disappearing and my being skinned alive. The world itself has its head in a bag. No book is going to reveal clues bit by bit as it's being read. It's up to us to write the book indefinitively, to lead the world up the garden path, so to speak. Besides, aren't all of our stories a little farfetched, haven't we invented all of our stories ourselves?

THE fire that had burned in the stove and boiled the water that scalded me does not frighten me, though. In the village where I spent the month of June on vacation not long ago, there was a great midsummer's night celebration with a huge bonfire right in the middle of the square. When the pyre was in place and set alight, the flames leapt so high they looked like a tree. It was out of the question to jump over the fire while it was still so spirited, so violent; we had to wait until it calmed down a bit. At best we would race through it, and tradition had it that a few show-offs, four or five at most, no doubt already tipsy, would take the risk, greeted on the other side with blankets held out to them by the firefighters. Under the mocking eyes of my very virile companions, I also stepped forward to cross the fire, which I did without any apprehension, like someone miraculously cured of the plague who could parade among the stricken, certain she would not catch it a second time. No one tried to dissuade me, I probably looked very determined, but I did not take the basic precaution of splashing myself with water beforehand and when I rejoined my friends, their astonished faces told me that my hair, at least the front of it, along with my eyebrows and lashes, were like dry straw that fell when I shook. It wasn't terribly serious, didn't people used to burn the ends of their hair in order to grow more abundant locks? Everything grew back quite quickly, in fact. By keeping silent, the show-offs had taken a little revenge for my intrusion (or perhaps they were too drunk to notice anything?). As for me, I had been pretty careless not to inquire about anything and to believe that the men had wet hair from splashing one another at the water fountain in a simple after-drinking game. It wasn't terribly serious, and was even quite comical. My bangs had not only burned, but they stood straight up in a stiff, farcical tuft. The midsummer fire episode became a kind of ridiculous subplot of my forgotten burns, like in ancient times in the bull ring, when the poor horses of the picadors, grotesquely gored by the bull, are theatrically evacuated from the arena while the real tragedy is being prepared.

To be honest, in my story fire is only a mediator. It was water that burned me. On the whole, I have managed to make amends with fire, but the same cannot be said for water. Even cold, completely cold, it always worries me. Although I love the sight of the sea, only a strong heat wave will make me go for a swim. And even then I have to force myself a little. I am all the more captivated by the grace of the cuttlefish unfurling its long hair in the waters because I will never understand it, whatever understanding it may be. Unless I eat it. Eating cuttlefish, is that not in fact wanting to appropriate a little of its grace (the way people once thought that eating your enemy's liver gave you his strength) and triumph over the fear it causes me, the cuttlefish and its kingdom of water. I remember the pleasure I got from eating crocodile one day in Australia. I also remember when I was a child the sudden decision my grandmother made to kill and cook a rooster that had jumped in my face one morning when I walked into the hen house. She served it to us at lunch time and I ate heartily. Never had a sentence seemed more just. The next morning I walked into the hen house without fear. The other roosters had to behave themselves, for hadn't I intimately experienced what had become of a rooster's arrogance?

BURN your wings, burn the midnight oil, burn the candle at both ends, burn with impatience, burn with love, you, burn, burn, burn. Burn your boats so you reach an extreme, a limit, the margin, from where you return, if you return, forever changed, pierced, altered, grown, weighed down, lightened, I don't know, but changed. By burning myself, I touched the other side, "You're burning!" cried all the dead, who are not without humor. Perhaps that is why I count on the living to welcome me and to reiterate again and again their signs of welcome. For once you have touched the other side, you can easily slide in without even noticing. On the other side, once we've touched it, they recognize us with the slightest inadvertence. They take us by our feet, pulling softly, gently, so we can do nothing but let ourselves go; perhaps despite ourselves we take a liking to the other side, at least they no longer scare us as much, yes, that's it, we realize with horror that they don't scare us as much as they should. Hey! Hey the living! Hold us by the hand, hold us back or we'll sink straight to the bottom. Don't we already look like someone who's drowned?

DROWNED in boiling water that, flowing over you, marks your skull with the baptism of the dead. It's an invisible tonsure that forever parts your hair. It quite soberly announces the barbarous baptism that lapped the back of your head, the nape of your neck, your entire body, that peeled you alive, turned you inside out like a glove, like an octopus, to see what you were worth underneath, that ravaged, mangled, and turned you crimson, that cooked and blistered you and your memory as well, that ate up your nightmares and suffering and left nothing behind but a tiny circle of skin, an infinitely derisory circle where no hair grows. And so to the saucepan where the cuttlefish and onions again simmer, I add two good splashes of cognac, I let it all warm up and then I remove the saucepan from the heat (it's very important to remove the saucepan from the heat, otherwise the flambé could become dangerous and we all know that we don't like dangerous games). I immediately strike a match and bring it near the surface of the dish. *Poof!* the flame rises and dances on the burning cognac until all the alcohol is gone. For a few seconds the flame is not under the dish but above it like a crowning glory, a nimbus above what is cooked, to death transformed (as one would say about a try in rugby).

I WOULD dream about a painting where there was no question of drowning, or burning, or dangerous games, or anything that touched me closely, dream about a painting in which I didn't recognize myself, dream about a painting in which I could lose myself, dream about a painting that was soft without being obscure, that was soft without being limp, dream about a painting that was soft or, rather, that was pacified, that had passed through violence, that had known it well and had taken it in, that had shouldered it, engulfed it, made it its own to the point that the consumed violence became an iron lance of softness, its secret armor, the one that would back softness into a corner, the one that would make softness split open like a peach and spill its refreshing juice, I would dream about a painting that would not be a big blaze, but whose ardent affability would seep into you like a warm gust of wind.

ingredients being added with a sort of impatience, almost irritation. Most important, once again place the saucepan over the heat, so the cooking takes matters into its own hands. So it takes off, so it starts smoking, for God's sake! And then *wham! bam!* the white wine, a full glass, with gusto.

THE cuttlefish that were just licked by the fragile blue flame (an angel passed by), are now cooking full steam ahead. Now is not the time to sink into idleness. The alcohol from the white wine must vigorously sing itself hoarse. Then we lower the heat. It smells good. An extraordinarily familiar smell, despite the cuttlefish, of good things that simmer and whet the appetite. The foreignness of the cuttlefish with its crowned head has been tucked away in the kitchen's pocket. I think of stronger smells. Of one I smelled in a house in the village, not far from Claire's in fact, where they were making green tomato preserves. I don't remember now what I was doing in that house, but I do remember the smell of cat piss and of the stuffiness that crowded the hallway carpeted with bags, crates, and piles of newspaper. When the door opened, the smell of that unknown preserve gushed forth and immediately erased the rather sickening stench of the long-accumulated junk. It was almost like opening a window to the living smell of the sea. I had no

10.

Add white wine, garlic, *bouquet garni,* parsley, tomato purée, salt and pepper

THINGS are picking up a little. The dish has more or less taken shape. Now it is time to season it, which is just as essential as getting it underway. One cannot lose sight of this, what follows is not the cherry on top or even the finishing touch. Relatively speaking, what follows is more like putting the boat we have just built into the water. It means not losing the rhythm that held sway when the dish was first made. And maybe even the opposite, of amplifying the rhythm, making quicker, hastier gestures as though we were running out of time or as though the success of the dish depended on things being dealt with quickly, on idea you could make preserves from tomatoes and, what's more, from tomatoes that hadn't yet ripened. So far, I had only seen women choose fruit that was the ripest, sometimes overripe, and cook it for long periods of time. Those tomatoes, still spry, gave off an acidic smell that evoked the scent of lemons, but it didn't dazzle like fresh, healthy citrus fruit. The smell of cooking green tomatoes, cut into slices and dipped in sugar, was smoother and heavier, much more intoxicating than the scent of lemons. It locked in the heartiness that the tomatoes would have had if they had matured and thus would have spread around more thickly. But this aroma was infinitely more compressed and in an instant it absorbed you sharply and completely with the impertinence of one that hasn't faded in the slightest. It caught in your nose and the back of your throat and didn't let go for quite some time. So that to me, the expression "stick your nose where it doesn't belong" is meaningless since my nose is reserved for smells I have smelled lovingly. I also think of the first small fire we made in the yard once the summer heat had died down and no longer prohibited our cut grass, our branches, and our gathered undergrowth from going up in smoke. That fire was not without nostalgia since it certified that summer was truly over, but it softened the little taste of sadness it placed on our tongues by warming up the evenings that were already starting to cool down, and its pungency made a beautiful blaze out of melancholy itself.

I THINK of stronger odors but at the same time the smell of my steaming dish covers everything, penetrates the clothing, hair, inundates the house to such an extent that I seem to detect in my dish the scent of the green tomato preserves and the first fire in the yard at summer's end. It has often seemed to me, it's true, that a sensation, provided it is felt strongly enough, contains many other, if not all, sensations, as though they were interwoven, flowed from one into the other and were held together tightly like cut-out dolls that appear once you unfold the paper. In short, it has often seemed to me that what matters most is the presiding intensity of sensation, as opposed to its actual properties. *Sensation,* the word is just as annoying as the word *atmosphere* bleated by that comedienne Arletty. Like her, we, too, would like to deform and twist it so that it loses the haze that surrounds it, so that it is defined with the clean cut of a knife and jabs us between the ribs, so that the sensation rids us of the thickness of our blood.

IN the meantime, let's peel more garlic, three cloves for good measure, with its unripe, musky odor, both acidic and warm, that my parents didn't like and that I loved to soak up when Madame Pignon, the burly grocer, gave us garlic toast for a treat (it seemed, though, that we only got the smell of garlic, since she merely rubbed the clove across the bread that was sprinkled with olive oil and then put in the oven). My father especially noticed right away that I had eaten garlic and declared that the smell made him sick, it reminded him of the strong smell of sweat and I don't know what else that's dirty and repugnant. He vindicated his anger by accusing Madame Pignon of giving children things to eat when she was "slightly questionable." And garlic, like her, was slightly questionable in the eyes of my father. It drew me into intimacy with a foreignness that my father literally could not abide and that he must have felt in a vague sort of way detached me from him. But however much Madame Pignon was slightly questionable, and however many warts, some hairy at that, covered her face, I never saw her as the witch my father made her out to be. By opening the doors of her jet black oven where all sorts of savory tarts were baking and by giving us the garlic-rubbed bread, she opened the doors to the unknown and the unknown smelled so wonderful that it could not have been entirely bad. As for witches, I knew *they* didn't open *anything*; they imprison, they lock children up, sometimes even in their oven, in order to cook them like the witch who lured Hansel and Gretel into her gingerbread house with the sugar-glazed windows. Witches don't teach children to like strong and powerful things, they get them all sticky with candy.

MY parents did reach the fragrant darkness of that foreign place, the blazing fire of the unknown by means of little herbs. We often need these viatica, a few last words, a rosary, a candle or two to help us across the chasm. Those little herbs didn't have the candor of garlic and were perhaps less frightening because of it. They grew naturally along familiar lanes, among a number of other things that smelled as powerfully as they did. They ended up imposing themselves on us with their patience, by dint of growing just about anywhere. Tonight I am tying them into a bouquet, a sort of homage to their modesty. But along those friendly lanes where the knowledge of thyme, savory, and rosemary is foraged, I once again fall to my knees. Nothing will happen tonight. Nothing will happen and I won't be able to stop myself from waiting for something to happen. I could kick myself for waiting, it's not becoming, it's not cool, it's not good at all. I'm all nerves. Will they see that I'm waiting? Will I be burdensome? Or just the opposite, will they see nothing at all? Will I be up to expectations? Will I be too flippant? Quite simply, will I be up to this dinner I'm hosting? I tie up my bouquet of laneway scents and a few bay leaves with some kitchen thread and set it in the casserole with all the care of a funeral director.

I HAVE some parsley left, already pressed, a sprinkle of parsley. And the little can of tomato purée, open, with a dome of purée still stuck to the lid that we sometimes swipe and lick off our index finger. It's actually not that good, but it has always been irresistible. The consistency, the color. Whoever has never licked anything while cooking can cast the first stone. Cooking exalts, irritates, calms, and reconciles me. Bores and enchants. Disgusts. Never ceases to surprise. So many colors, smells, consistencies to infinitely intertwine. So many tastes to fit together, to extract, so many tastes to extol, to bend to our will, to convince to swell, and to anoint our mouths. So many rules, so many habits, so many surprises. Cooking makes me despair. Sometimes I don't understand a thing. What do I have to do with it? Is it an infatuation? Who do I feel like treating to such a delicious meal? What am I trying to pull? Sometimes it seems that cooking gives me a bit of relief from violence. And I rebel. I insist on my violence, which I deplore, like I take to the apple of my eye. I don't like fussy eaters; on the contrary, I like when people eat heartily, with lots of appetite. But at the same time I believe that cooking relieves me of my voraciousness. Cooking civilizes me and I hate cooking because it civilizes me. Cooking and its corollary, civility. The most surly face breaks into a smile if what you have cooked is to his liking and you hear yourself saying to the person you've disliked since the evening began, "Have some more, please, it's my pleasure." Nor would you cook just for yourself. When you imagine a dish, you immediately think of the people you would invite to share it. Isn't it strange that you who seem to prize your solitude above all else find yourself for hours at a time at your stove and, to be more precise, entirely devoted to the people who will soon eat your meal? No doubt you wish to astonish them with your cooking, those who are about to taste your meal, unless it is you yourself that you astonish, unless it is you yourself that you end up primping and dressing up in order to make yourself presentable when you speak to them. Your raw face, they won't see it; your raw words, they won't hear them. Your raw face and words would be too frightening and too magnificently lost for anyone to ever see or hear. Even *you* cannot maintain them. They scarcely belong to you anymore and almost drag you away, far away, to where the sea is not frozen with spiked, motionless waves, to where the sea sweeps along the dead and the living alike, jumbled together, to where there is nothing in the sea but the fervor of its movement.

THERE, in the yellow light of the early evening, the cook from *Alice* reappears, enormous and grumbling, a gigantic pepper mill in her hand that is thick and red, perpetually grinding her pepper, ferociously, as though she were grinding fury itself, flying all around her and causing her to sneeze with great gusto. Luckily, she crops up every once in a while. Otherwise we might think that cooking was nothing but delicate, sophisticated, meticulous work. The cook wielding her formidable temperament has perfect timing, arriving at the moment of pepper and salt to remind us that cooking can also lapse a little into raciness, crudeness, exaggeration, maybe a little into bulging and even ugliness, into what grimaces and bloats, into the devouring ogre who fills people with fright. Grinding away with a great sweep of her arm at the pepper, whose dust gives her a halo and trails after her like the twinkling tail of a comet, the cook barrels down on us, knocks us aside without further ado, armed, not only with her pepper mill, but with the incredible bustle of apron, skirt, and petticoat, insults and cries of rage; we founder like miserable Lilliputians, who are shaking with laughter, hiccups, and the fear that, despite everything, the cook will smother us beneath the circus big top of her dubiously white clothes.

11.

Slip in a bit of cayenne pepper (or, according to taste, 1 to 3 bird peppers)

HERE I opt for the parenthesis, the bird peppers, not for the taste, but because I cannot claim to know the difference between cayenne pepper and bird pepper, which even to look at, are as alike as two peas in a pod, oblong and red, one tending more to orange and the other to brown. Not for taste, but because cayenne peppers are harder to find. Besides, I already had a small jar of bird peppers in my cupboard that I must have bought for the name. I carefully take three peppers out of the jar. They look like little tongues, but they are nothing like the tongue you would proudly stick out, nothing like the tongue with which you lash out, so to speak, furtively, at your adversary. They are brownish, as I said, and quite withered and dry like old people's skin. I can't help but imagine three birds holding these ill-suited tongues tightly in their beaks. They protrude strangely, they protrude too far, elongating the bird in a grotesque and disturbing way. It's only by biting the pepper that the bird truly appears, singing its cheerful, breathtaking song. The bird-tongue pepper should be bitten; you have to suffer a bit as though you were biting your own tongue, but the blood that gushes from the pepper makes the mouth sing non-stop. Although the mouth is closed, the tongue expands as though someone had raised a curtain to discover a stage, while cheeks redden and eyes water a bit. The bird-tongue, pointed yet crumpled, stings where it should. It titillates, it ferrets out, it whips, it interferes from below, it laps up, it grates, it doesn't miss a crumb, it contrives. To your tongues, dear guests, let us give some tongue, tongue that burns, the bird tongue, the viper tongue, the cat tongue, let's lick up every drop, let's taste from the tip of the tongue, let's loosen, fork, bite our tongues, let's crudely cluck our tongues as we would before a choice morsel, let's click our tongues loudly, be extreme, stop smiling thinly without showing our teeth and stick out our big, eager tongues, our famished, blue tongues, our heavy-drinking tongues, our secret, piggish tongues, our firebrand tongues, our thick ogre and ogress tongues, our multiple tongues burgeoning like the arms of a squid, stick out our spiteful tongues, the hideous one, the bitch, and even stick out our nice and sweet tongues, wrapped in warm saliva and use them, these nice and sweet tongues, to lick one another with the utmost care right down to our toes. Let's stop talking about one thing or another, let's stop talking obscenely about the bad things in the world, let's stop talking shamelessly, casually over coffee about the world whose throat we're slitting and rather, let's stuff our tongue in the mouth of whoever piques our appetite the most. And so let's twirl our tongues around seven times in the mouth of whoever arouses us the most and shut up for goodness sake. Let's drop all this coquetry, violently tangle our tongues and finish by pulling back, with aching tongues, short of breath, with disheveled hair and the crimson flush of a drunk. We will then doubly enjoy the taste of the stuffed cuttlefish, the delicately spiced taste we ravenously seize from the tongue of our guest. Delicately, for what is even more disturbing is that the bird-tongue pepper must be *slipped* in. What gesture is needed for this enigmatic slipping? No question of stuffing the peppers into three of the little bundled bodies. They would be too spicy and the others not spicy enough, and three of the guests would risk being more ruffled than the rest of the table, even choked with surprise. Just what is this gesture we are invited to make? How do we *slip* the peppers into the sauce? Perhaps furtively, as though there were some danger to this addition? In the end, however, I decide that this was nothing more than a coquettish whim on the part of the my neighbor who dictated the recipe to me; I toss the peppers into the sauce. Of course, slipping or no slipping, we'll see nothing but fire. The peppers tossed in, I think that rather than slip my tongue into my favorite guest's mouth, I'd like our gazes to meet and open up so widely that they no longer belong to any one of us, but become like a bouquet whose subtle red flowers would be our smiles and our smiles would join end to end without touching in the slightest as they draw us skyward from the earth.

12.

Simmer for approximately ¾ of an hour

HERE it is, almost finished, my excitement still hasn't died down and even the seasoning has been checked, several times, readjusted; didn't I go too fast, didn't I just throw everything together? There would almost be time to start all over again, the wait seems endless until they arrive. And yet I have dozens of things to get ready, the appetizers, dessert, and the table, not to mention my outfit, a little makeup, my hair. But the main event of this dinner is without a doubt the stuffed cuttlefish. The extras leave me cold. Here it is, almost finished. I could have gone on all night. But at the same time, cooking could soon have made me sick; being glued to the saucepan and the stove that flushes my cheeks, confined to this room like my mother and my grandmother before her, I think about a magnificent somewhere else, lofty journeys, storybook explorations, sometimes I think back to when I was young, loved, adored, basking in the hopes that were inevitably placed in me and I feel like crying, how true it is that we only ever cry for ourselves—look at the platitudes we manage to trot out when we cook—and yet, how can we truly believe in a magnificent somewhere else, lofty journeys, storybook explorations? Wouldn't I also feel like crying? Alone in the middle of the beautiful raging sea, thinking back to when I was young, loved, adored, it's true that deep down, I feel closer to those who look to their houses, even to their saucepans, so why cry, I feel so volatile, so unwise despite the recent appearance of one or two gray hairs; I remember having been more so, there is no progress, no advancement, only fits and starts of enlightenment and then the backsliding that sometimes takes us five or ten years to get over. Still, be careful to watch that it doesn't cook too quickly, that it doesn't stick, done, done, easy to say, but if it didn't cook like it was supposed to, everything would be ruined. I will cook it, as I said, longer than the recipe recommends, a good hour, maybe even a bit longer, I am still rather wary of the rubbery texture of the cuttlefish mantles. I have all the time I need to get ready. I don't think I'll wear that overly enticing dress; no, in the end, something simpler, something not too stimulating to the eye, not too distracting, so that my secret love, if he comes, sees my secret hair, so that my love, known only to me, sees my hair known only to him, while the other guests pay us fluttering court and our gazes do not grow heavy because of it. Over an hour, I have plenty of time to comb my invisible hair so it spreads out for my hidden love, to style it at length with harsh and soft words, to smooth it, soothe it, let it fly away like a mythological horse, over an hour, plenty of time, plenty of time carved out like a deep tunnel inexplicably paved with light in this unique hour when day tilts dangerously and begins to spill over into night. Over an hour, anxious and slow, while the dish that will delight my love simmers, for of course it was prepared only for the ring I slipped into it, that only he can find and that he'll show me between his teeth, unbeknownst to the others, and that he'll clasp between his teeth—the ring that I slid in just for him, shiny and quivering even more than the tongue of a kiss. We are visitors, visitors to ourselves; the angel who visits me, and who *is* me as well, knows how to talk to the angel of my love, she slips her slender tongue through the ring clasped between the teeth of my love's angel and they both laugh in full flight. Right after, my love and I talk of this and that, we haven't forgotten that a second or two earlier, we were drinking each other, we were drinking the marvelous water that flowed between our teeth, we haven't forgotten, but the curtain has fallen. Sometimes we are between the two angels, our arms still slipped through the angels', and we can even feel the warm pressure, though we are already talking about other things, the affairs of the world that we barely understand, so that, more than usual, we hear the sound of our voices like the voices of others, more than usual, we hear our voices detaching themselves from our mouths and in spite of ourselves get all worked up, and this makes us feel ashamed and a little bit scared, it's as though these usurped voices violate our mouths, as though the words don't come out where they should, that they squeeze over to one side of the mouth, that our mouths then become crooked, cluttered with speech that can't find the right path, that our mouths are slightly paralyzed, almost painfully so, and if we continue to talk it's against our will, but the wine is flowing, isn't it, what we nevertheless fear more than anything is that these voices so unlike our own will suddenly dry up, even dry up all voices, even the voice of the angel, even the voice that finds the right path, so that we can never again utter a single word, our sewn-up mouths, scarred mouths, burned mouths, we fear above all that one day the scars of our buried burns will end up peeling back our skin as though what had been growing until now is nothing but an exuberantly painful and monstrous excrescence, beyond all wounds, beyond pain, and that the price to be paid should be the barrage of our mouths, their erasure, sewn-up mouths, sealed, basted hastily, so that justice be done without further ado, so that justice be rendered to the little burned body huddled inside us, more forgotten than the most forgotten recluse. Here it is, already finished, simmering almost without me, barely two or three turns with the wooden spoon, casually; I'd like to fall asleep in the comforting aroma that wafts around, a familiar smell overpowered by the scent of tomatoes cooking gently and coddling the memory, I'd like to fall asleep to the susurrant murmur of the simmering stuffed cuttlefish, I'd like to sink straight to the bottom and slumber in the hollow of the sheet where the angel and the others who speak in my place and hurl abuse no longer recognize each other, tangled up more tightly than underbrush, where the unintelligible words of falling asleep have one and the same voice, barely audible, a wisp of a voice, barely a voice, but more mine perhaps for not knowing who it is meant for, and thus not calculating, not considering or anticipating, knowing nothing of its effects, not knowing for whom it is meant, but still ardently meant, ardently uttered, a wisp of a voice where my secret love and the love of my love and my lost loves would be contained, a wisp of a voice that is inconsolable and yet silently inflated by desire, a wisp of a voice where all the voices that speak in my place would be mixed together, I would like to sleep so this song has a chance to leave me, this tiny song, this slow and fragile melody. Something simpler, yes, not an overly enticing dress, I could just as easily have wanted the opposite, for how could my love feel ill-at-ease with even a garish dress and why wouldn't I throw my love to the world as though I were on my balcony and everyone could see me; love also gives you these kinds of yearnings, to be arrogant, stormy, ready to fight, irrational, to acquire a taste for commotion, challenge; love produces these kinds of childish yearnings and the yearning to be humble, to develop a taste for challenge, provocation, and even commotion, you mustn't mistake them, the yearning to denounce oneself, to be modest, effaced, it will be beautiful, it will be magnificent, I select, for good this time, the red dress, better to strut around than to play the pious hypocrite, "you are not modest," says the old woman from Stromboli to Ingrid Bergman, noisily rolling the "r" in "are," splendid and awkward, like my love, like the love of my love, my volcano, my sweetness, one night in a boat we actually passed right by the volcano on Stromboli Island, the earth was naively sending stars into the sky the way a child sends kisses with her hand, we told the sky about the burning that consumes us, you are not modest, to which is added the pride that our immodesty spits in our faces and banishes us. It was beautiful, it was magnificent, on the deck of that boat, from the darkness of the sea, we looked to where the stars were scattered, an upside-down shower of stars, we sailed across the sky and the sea gently rinsed the summer night, my volcano, my sweetness, let's take off these old clothes, let's put on that red dress that we still haven't worn, let's go a little overboard, let's put on makeup, let's carefully style our hair, let's use creams and perfumes and oils, let the cooking continue, let's devour each other with our eyes, my volcano, my sweetness, my love that sends stars to the sky, my love blown out of proportion the way I'm taken in by the enchanting words, the way I love you because you devour me with your appetite, almost greedily, yes greedily, as though you were afraid to go without, as though you couldn't stop yourself from pouncing on the food, despite the bad impression, bad manners, as though you couldn't stop rudely wiping your plate clean to the last drop of sauce and asking for more, I love you for your unrefined candor, for your piggishness, for your puppy-like impatience, I love you as you devour me and relentlessly sink in your wolf fangs, half dog, half wolf, in the dusk of the evening, we are at the uncertain hour of twilight when we don't know whether to choose the day side or the night side, we sense that something is lying in wait, that something is suspended we don't quite know what, but it seems that we acquire a sort of benevolence, quite temporarily, that we pour into the night for good, a sort of benevolence that makes us willing to love everything, to mock nothing, we're willing to forgive everything while we ourselves are so ambivalent, so unsteady, hopping from one foot to the other like a frantic child. Most important, it shouldn't stick; the slightest hint of burned food would destroy everything, and none of those rough errors worthy of the most ignorant or worse, the most careless of beginners, keep watch right up to the end and do not think that it's finished, we often extol the beginnings, but let's keep the fervor of the beginning until the end, now here's another story altogether, this should draw some attention, may the end be like the beginning or, even better, may the end *be* a beginning, may the discouragement and excitement of the start never cease to intertwine like the feet of secret lovers under the table, and for the guests who see only fire, may the appetite always rise from its ashes, despite the sickness, fatigue, and sleep that nips treacherously at the nape of the neck, I'd fall asleep in a wink, I'd let sleep make its nest on my belly and hang its undergrowth from my hair, in a wink I'd no longer be there for anyone and at the same time I fidget with impatience, I fidget, I fidget as I wait for my guests, wait for them to unknowingly escort the one among them I prefer, for them to make an innocent procession to my heart's desire, sounding imaginary trumpets, nonchalantly wrapped in colorful cloth like no other, I fall asleep and fidget, I take my red dress out of the wardrobe so everyone can see me and nothing will suit me more than being as transparent as the breath of an angel, hidden in the wardrobe that held the dress, buried, vanished, don't think we'll catch you, right? That we're waiting for you around the corner, that we're waiting where we think we'll find you and where you go to great lengths not to be found, cuttlefish for squid, cuttlefish for calamari, and all the hair so mixed up, so muddled, so entangled that no comb will ever again be able to separate the strands. Tangled, knotted, entwined hair. What does *my love* mean, what does *I love you* mean if not perhaps that the words surge at the same time as something else surges in the chest. Does the word *love* not come to the lips to prevent other words from swelling disproportionately, so that they don't explode in every direction and so that in the end, we aren't left only with exhausted scraps, drained of all the breath needed to inflate them, *my love* to say calmly that we are beside ourselves? It's strange that in order to find the right words, the words that fit, you need calm and a kind of passion, perhaps even fury; I think of soufflés, of cakes magnificently risen in the oven, I think of the patience required to make them, elevated, exhausted, in the furious heat of the oven, I think of beaten egg whites, the whites shaken with rage until they lose their pathetic phlegm white consistency and reach the ineffable solidity of snow; it's strange that at the same time you need constancy and fever and that *constancy* and *fever,* so seemingly distant at first glance, lean on each other and support each other like two merry-makers at the end of a wedding. My stuffed cuttlefish simmers over low heat. Who will truly taste it, I mean with his mouth cleansed of all that it has tasted before, who will truly taste it, his mouth cleansed like a lover would have done, taking the utmost care with his or her toilet and rinsing his or her mouth at length, whoever truly tastes it will find the ring I slid in. And when the ring is found by whoever truly tasted it, wings will grow on both our backs. The ring has been rubbed so many times, teeth have almost seized it so many times. Once, teeth even bit into it without realizing and the tongue was already going to wet it, but the teeth loosened their grip and the ring fell back, drunk and lost for a long time; I have made incantations so many times, *my love* and other words I've forgotten, so many times the ring I slid into my cooking has not been found. For the next hour, I will once again lower the heat under the saucepan that, ever since my childhood when I stood stock still in front of the neighbor's stove, when my curiosity bound me to the lair (but a surprisingly luminous lair) of Cinderella's Godmother, I see, like a boat capsized in the infinite aromas of the world, as though the unknown of the world were woven there, fermenting in the murkiness of the slips and inventing itself there; in the next hour I will carefully turn once or twice more the mantles of the cuttlefish that are slowly cooking; in the next hour I will expect nothing or next to nothing of the upcoming evening, but I can't stop myself from letting my hair grow like Mélisande, my invisible and magnificent hair, it is massive and it pulls me backward, it wouldn't take much for it to topple me over, in the next hour I'll take a shower until the most hidden, the most loving strands of my hair are flooded.